THE
GOD
PARTICLE

THE
GOD
PARTICLE

VALENTINE L. KRUMPLIS

Order this book online at www.trafford.com
or email orders@trafford.com

Most Trafford titles are also available at major online book retailers.

Printed in the United States of America.

ISBN: 978-1-4669-3784-0 (sc)
ISBN: 978-1-4669-3783-3 (e)

Trafford rev. 05/17/2012

www.trafford.com

North America & international
toll-free: 1 888 232 4444 (USA & Canada)
phone: 250 383 6864 ♦ fax: 812 355 4082

SCENE 1

Chicago, Michigan Avenue. A good looking man in his thirties is entering an office building. He goes to a board where he is looking at the listings in the building. He looks, and the camera focuses in on a name, Dr. Philip Fishbein, suite 2121. The man proceeds to the elevator and goes up to the twenty first floor. He goes down the corridor and enters a reception room 2121. Inside is a little old lady, the receptionist.

RECEPTIONIST
    Can I help you?

VISITOR
    I do not think YOU can help me, but the doctor might be able.

RECEPTIONIST
    You have an appointment?

VISITOR
    Yes, my name is Peter Metcalf.

RECEPTIONIST
    Yes, we have you on the list here at eleven in the morning. I will tell the doctor you are here.

PETER
    Thank you.

The receptionist buzzes the doctor and announces that Mr. Metcalf is here. A few moments later Peter is shown into the doctor's office.

DOCTOR
    Hello Mr. Metcalf, or can I call you Peter?

PETER
    Peter is fine doctor.

The doctor is a thin man has a tan and also sports a pony tail of graying hair.

DOCTOR
    Well Peter first let me ask you if you would like the couch or the chair for our discussion.

PETER

Chair is fine doctor.

DOCTOR

Let me tell you about myself, first, Peter so that we can better understand my methods.

I graduated from University of Illinois with a doctorate in Psychology in 1963. I then got a medical degree in Mexico, and got certified in the states. I am a firm believer that any problems or questions you may have we can clarify by using my methods I developed over the years. I believe all the answers, frustrations, depressions, are hidden in our own minds, all we have to do is dig them out.

PETER

Well I hope you are right. I do need a reality check. I need to know what is happening to me. Strange things are happening.

DOCTOR

You see first we sort the problems out. We label them. Some are chemical and require medicine. These are various depressions and other chemical imbalances. These problems can, most of the times be fixed by drugs, or cocktails of drugs. The second set of problems is the imagined type. Reality here is distorted by the brain not able to process information properly. People in this group imagine situations, they possibly believe the world will end soon or the government is doing something to hurt them. Many variations of fantasies are in this group. Science does not know if it is a chemical imbalance or just the brain is wired wrong. Reality is lost on this group. I try to wire the brain correctly through therapy.

PETER

Well this is what I need, as I told you. I need a reality check. The question I have for you, is how you decide on what is real?

DOCTOR

I am not the decider like our ex president Bush. I am more a referee of facts and fantasies that you may have. I work with you to prove or disprove what you state.

PETER

In your career have you ever found illusions or fantasies to be true?

DOCTOR

No, but I have lost patients who continue in their illusions. Reality was not forthcoming.

PETER

When I talked to you making the appointment, I told you I was having out of body experiences.

DOCTOR

I noted that and I had several cases of people claiming to be able to leave their bodies. Astral travel I believe. I prescribed pills for them to stop traveling.

PETER

My out of body travel is so real that I can prove it to you. I am sure I can convince you I can do this. It is not an illusion. I need from you to understand what I can do and then tell me that I am not insane, imagining this. The problem within me is that I can do what is not real, yet I know reality is also here, so how do I connect these two?

DOCTOR

Tell me how you see this out of body travel working and when did it start?

PETER

When I go to sleep I find myself fully awake and I can transport myself to different locations that I choose to imagine.

DOCTOR

You wrote in your file that this started, the dreams, while you were in the hospital recovering from your car accident. I also understand you were pronounced dead and then resuscitated. You were also diagnosed as being paralyzed. Must be some good hospital you were in.

PETER

Hospital was fine, I was really dead for a brief moment but thanks to a persistent Doctor Mustafa he kept working on me and brought me back.

DOCTOR

That happens sometimes. This doctor Mustafa then also believed you were paralyzed and treated you.

PETER

I was paralyzed and he treated me with some stem cell derivatives that were not approved in this country.

DOCTOR

Tell me about the accident.

PETER

I was driving home from Kalamazoo to Chicago. I had made a bunch of sales call there. There was a snow storm, I was speeding and clipped a snow plow. I was also on the phone at that time and went off the road and hit some trees.

DOCTOR

I guess this is a good reason not to talk on the phone. What do you sell by the way?

PETER

I sell toilet paper and other paper products.

DOCTOR

I am sorry to keep asking you these seemingly irrelevant questions but there are a lot of clues in this. How do you FEEL as a college graduate having to sell toilet paper?

PETER

You clean up the brain I clean up the other end. I never felt somehow less of a person selling ass wipe. What does that have to do with my problem?

DOCTOR

You had no desire to be something more than you were? No great frustration to be something else?

PETER

No.

DOCTOR

So you wake up in the hospital and find yourself paralyzed.

PETER

Correct.

DOCTOR

What happens next?

PETER

My wife Janet is there and tells me how lucky I am to be alive. She tells me that my file contains documentation stating that I had been diagnosed as dead but the one doctor would not give up and kept trying to bring me back. Janet also tries to lie to me about the paralysis from the neck down. I tell her I can not feel anything or move anything.

DOCTOR

So here you are walking, so I guess the hospital misdiagnosed you on the paralysis also.

PETER

I was paralyzed and I had been dead. I even received the last rites from a Father Cinikas. I do not mind the last rites even tho I consider myself more an agnostic than a Catholic.

DOCTOR

So we have to admit that you were mentally traumatized. Very upset with the belief you were possibly, permanently paralyzed.

PETER

I knew I was paralyzed. I was thirty three years old and now I had to be a vegetable for another fifty or sixty years. I wished I was dead. You can not imagine the horror of living with my reality. You can not move, you can not scratch, you can not piss, you can not shit, you can never fuck again. Your mind is completely possessed by an unimaginable depression. You wish for death.

DOCTOR

But here you are today being able to do everything. You should then be grateful to God for this miracle.

PETER

It was not any God but doctor Mustafa with his illegal stem cell drugs that cured me, he knew how miserable I was and secretly dosed me with them.

DOCTOR

So you believe you were not misdiagnosed, but that these drugs somehow connected your severed nerves.

PETER

All I know is, I begged doctor Mustafa to give me the drugs after he hinted he had a procedure that might help but was not legal. I convinced Janet to also ask him to help me.

The treatment took a year and I stopped believing in it and plunged into depressions. I put everyone through hell.

DOCTOR

You mentioned that the dreams started during the treatment when I talked to you on the phone.

PETER

Yes they did. Mustafa became concerned that the stem cell drugs were giving me side effects. He tried to explain that the drugs were not tested but he was seeing some response in my body to the drugs. I began to hate all the restrictions and the religious fools that set restrictions on stem cell research. I felt we were like Dr. Frankenstein working in secret. My progress was slow, and my dreams began to scare me. My depression deepened and I began to wish I was someplace else. Then it happened . . . I was able to be someplace else when I went to sleep.

DOCTOR

Your mind was the only thing you could use and you started imagining things happening to you.

PETER

You could say that, here I was laying in my shitty diaper, waiting for some nurse or helper to clean my ass for the rest of my life, and all I could do is think. I talked to doctor Mustafa because he was feeling guilty about giving me illegal drugs. I reasoned that if the drug worked it was my right to be healthy versus some religious nut cases barring stem cell research because of their God illusions.

DOCTOR

So supposedly you are regaining some movement but your dreams and out of body stories are scarring doctor Mustafa.

PETER

The healing is progressing but the mind is beginning to freak out. I tell Janet and doctor Mustafa that I am getting better but my mental condition is getting worse. Mustafa decides to give me a brain scan at this time.

DOCTOR

So Mustafa is concerned about the side effects causing you hallucinations.

PETER

They are not hallucinations as I will show you. The MRI of the brain shows Mustafa what he has never seen before in a human brain. There seems to be super activity in different parts of the brain that normally is not present. At this time Mustafa thinks of stopping the treatment but I beg him to continue. I now begin to move around and am transferred to rehabilitation. The hospital believes I was misdiagnosed and was in some catatonic shock.

DOCTOR

You believe it was the stem cell drugs that cured you and the hospital is still in the dark. At this time your dreams as you call them are becoming more real and you are able to have these out of body experiences

PETER

I tell doctor Mustafa that I can control my dreams. I can go where I dream, where I want to go. He begins to freak out on me. He thinks that he has made me insane. I tell him that my body is functioning alright and I just have to figure out my dream situation. Doctor Mustafa tells me that the hospital confiscated his files and samples of his drugs after the weird MRI was made known. He believes now he will be charged with all kinds of crimes, and lose his medical license. I ask him where the file is. He tells me it is now in the administrator's office. I tell him to stop by the next day and to be calm. I dream myself into the office and leave with the file.

DOCTOR

Now you will tell me you dreamed your way into a locked office and got the file.

PETER

Correct, and I gave the whole file, the next day, to doctor Mustafa. He was speechless, thanked me, and said he was leaving. He could not be charged with anything if the whole file was missing. He told me he would call me at my home to see how I am doing. He saw my improvement and knew I would soon be released.

DOCTOR

Well Peter you have an interesting story. I feel we covered a lot of ground today and I feel you opened yourself up to a situation where a scientific test can help prove or disprove your claims.

PETER

I know what I can do, unless I am completely insane. You are the one that needs the proof. I need to understand how this is happening to me. I have not told you my other problems tied in with the out of body adventures.

DOCTOR

Over the weekend why not dream yourself into my office here. It is locked, so is the whole floor. I will leave a book on my desk and you tell me the title of the book on Monday when we meet in the cafeteria on the first floor in this building, at noon. I will buy you lunch.

PETER

Easy test, I will pass. See you Monday.

As Peter leaves the room the doctor goes to his book shelf and picks out a red cover book called Dante's Inferno. He sets the book on his desk and snickers.

SCENE 2

Takes place in a cafeteria coffee shop of the Doctor's office building. This is a scene where the doctor sits reading the paper, waiting for Peter Metcalf to show up for the Monday meeting. Peter walks in and approaches the doctor.

DOCTOR

Good morning Peter.

PETER

Morning

Peter reaches into a bag and pulls out a red book and hands it to the doctor.

DOCTOR

That is some trick Peter. I went to my office in the morning and saw that the book was gone.

PETER

No trick doctor, I told you what my dreams are doing to me, it is driving me to doubt what is real. Do you believe me now? I can travel out of body and go where I want and take what I want.

DOCTOR

Please sit down and tell me how you managed to get into my office and take my copy of. "Dante's Inferno"?

PETER

We made a deal Friday that I would be able to prove my claims if I could dream my way into your office and tell you the title of the book. I did all of that and more.
Now you tell me it was a trick. What happened to our deal?

DOCTOR

Our deal, our proof, was for you to somehow dream your way into my office and tell me the title of the book on my desk. Yes or no?

PETER

Yes, but I wanted to show you the real problem. I have the out of body travel dreams but I am able to do physical things, pick up physical things. I have been doing this for some time.

DOCTOR

Taking physical things in your dreams and finding them at home when you wake up. Peter you have to admit that this is hard for anyone to believe. The normal explanations would be that you are imagining things, you are perhaps sleep walking. You are forgetting where you have been when you are awake and picked something up and took it home.

PETER

You might be right if the articles I brought back were random junk, but I am bringing back jewelry, art objects, baseball cards, stamp albums, perfume, rare books, and money.

DOCTOR

You are not lying to me? I could see these items if I wanted to see?

PETER

Yes, of course. What I tell my doctor is privileged and you could not inform the police on me.

DOCTOR

Yes, it is all confidential. What does your wife say about the items?

PETER

She thinks I am a thief, like a cat burglar. She like you did not believe in out of body travel until I stared giving her money and jewelry. It took a lot of stuff to convince her.

DOCTOR

So you give her, according to you, stolen jewelry, money, how does she feel about that?

PETER

She, I believe has a streak of larceny in her, Janet loves me very much but I think she sees that the world owes her a little of something. My accident and the recovery process wiped out all of our savings, our equity in the house, and left us completely destitute. Our credit was ruined by the medical bills, our insurance was not enough. We were planning to start a family. I believe my wife became very bitter. We had to start all over. She feels life owes her some nice things before she gets old.

DOCTOR

So lets play the game by your rules. Your wife is an enabler for you. You go to places that are locked up, secured, have video surveillance, and you are not photographed. I also presume you set off alarms. So how do you explain that?

PETER

I am in and out in a few minutes, the alarms go off, the cops come and I am gone.

DOCTOR

What about the surveillance films?

PETER

That is the fun part of my escapades. I create masks of different movie, cartoon characters. One time it is Porky Pig, the next time it is Leatherface, from Chain Saw Massacre. Keeps everyone entertained. I am thinking of doing one with the Easter bunny, maybe a Santa Claus robbing a candy store.

DOCTOR

I think Peter you and your wife both need a reality check. Our next appointment is Friday at two in the afternoon. Please both of you come, I will charge only for one or none, depending if we could arrive at some truth.

PETER

I think maybe all of us need a reality check, you too doctor. I would recommend you stop by the downtown police precinct and ask about some odd burglaries. a whole series of them in fact.

DOCTOR

If I do that will you promise to work with me on more logical explanations?

PETER

Depending on what you find out I will promise, if you will promise to go there.

DOCTOR

We then have a deal to work toward reality, yes?

PETER

See you Friday.

Peter leaves the restaurant, doctor gets up, leaves some money on the table and walks out looking at the red book, Dante's Inferno, Doctor shakes his head as he is walking out.

SCENE 3

The doctor enters a typical police station. The normal hustle and bustle is taking place. Whores are being arrested and walk past the doctor making lewd tongue motions at him. Young gang bangers are walked in front of him. People on a bench are comforting a girl with ripped clothes. One strange Mexican is yelling in Spanish. The doctor makes his way to the center desk. A fat red faced sergeant with the name tag Stan Slutarewski has just finished sermonizing two of the whores, stops and looks at the doctor and says.

Sergeant Stan

Are you the John that got robbed by these two or the lawyer for them? (The sergeant points to the two smiling black whores)

Doctor

No my name is not john, I am a psychiatrist, my name is Doctor Philip Fishbein.

Sergeant Stan

Well doctor you have certainly come to the right place. This is the center of all bedlam. I am very busy, so, what is your complaint or question or will you attempt a communal cure here for all of us?

Doctor

I am doing a research project on odd types of crime that somehow escape logic.
Like someone releasing alligators that keep growing in sewers, and also disappearing objects from impossible places and situations.

Sergeant Stan

This is your lucky day, we just had a meeting a week ago and the captain set up a new squad to handle odds and ends that irritate everyone. We call it the X section. Detective Ron Duffy is in charge. He is sitting way in that corner (he points there and yells out) Hey Duffy there is a shrink to see you, finally. Almost everyone starts laughing in the office as the doctor walks to Duffy's desk. A fat man is sitting eating doughnuts from a box.

Doctor

Detective Duffy I presume?

Duffy

No, Livingstone, Dr. Livingstone lately taking a break from Africa. What the hell do you want? You just gave those assholes in the office more material to make fun of this section. They already tell everyone that I am in charge of the X Files.

DOCTOR

I guess I should not have said I am a psychiatrist and caused you a problem.

DUFFY

I have many problems, can I unburden myself? Did the Mayor send you? No. You See my little department is an experiment. Unsolvable cases that nobody wants, are given to a fat man with a squad of people that no one wants in their department. The mayor decided to make the police department as diversified as the population they serve. So I have very short people, gay people, cripples, too tall people. See the mayor feels that not all cops have to have guns, be on the street, there is a great need for office workers and they can be of any size or persuasion.

DOCTOR

Well I see your problems. Change is something we all dislike but I believe diver-sification is good. You get a much more varied approach to problem solving.

DUFFY

Have a doughnut. Doctor??

DOCTOR

Sorry I did not introduce myself, I am Doctor Philip Fishbein.

DUFFY

I am sorry too Doctor Fishbein. You see I am the butt of jokes here. I am constantly harassed by my coworkers, my own team is difficult to work with, I have cases that are impossible to solve.

As they are talking an extremely short black man and a very tall blonde woman walk up to the desk.

DUFFY

Doctor Fishbein these are two of my assistants. This is Maurice Ward and Ann Bic.

DOCTOR

Nice to meet you, Maurice, Ann.

MAURICE

Nice to meet you, are you here to solve the nut robbery cases?

ANN

Doctor (gives her hand to Dr.)

DOCTOR

I am here to study the weird cases as you say, I do not know if I can help you solve them.

DUFFY

(eating a doughnut) Have one doctor, it will not kill you right away maybe later. Or maybe you could join me in my plan B.

DOCTOR

What is plan B?

DUFFY

I like to eat doughnuts if I get a heart attack from the fat I can sue the doughnut makers, get money and retire. They are not warning me enough about their food. All the fast food places should hire guards to keep fat people out of their restaurants. To be more politically correct all citizens should have a card updated every month with their cholesterol score and show that at the fast food window.

ANN

Doctor do you see now, why we are what we are here. How can we help you?

DOCTOR

You can tell me about your weird cases.

DUFFY

Hey team, we can do better for the doctor than tell him. We can show and tell.

MAURICE

What Duffy means is that we have compiled all the surveillance videos in a computer program and tried to find similarities of the perpetrators.

DUFFY

Let us go to the viewing room (All four of them go to a separate room, a voice is heard, hey doc, you going to need three couches?)

ANN

Fuck you Rodriguez go eat some beans.

RODRIGUEZ

Hey Ann how do you spell you last name? Is it B,I, C or B,I,T,C,H.

(They enter the office and Maurice sets up the computer.)

DUFFY

On the big screen Maurice, please.

(The different scenes begin to appear in different locations. In the jewelry store a person appears in front of the camera, smashes a glass case takes some rings and vanishes from the camera. The person was wearing a Porky Pig mask. There are many scenes with different character masks. President Nixon mask, leatherface, big bird, vampire, wolfman.)

DUFFY

You see why everyone is laughing at my squad. When we have meetings on this, my friends ask me if I will sell popcorn at the show. The unique thing about all of them is that there is no sign of breaking in or breaking out when leaving, yet all the interior alarms were set off by the thief.

MAURICE

The problem is that the insurance companies feel that it is an inside job, a scam by the owners to rip off the insurance companies. They feel someone developed a virtual reality type computer program, a game, sold it to some stores, and are playing a hoax. The insurers feel that the owners hide the missing objects then want to collect on them. A computer to camera integrated program is used.

ANN

It looks that way except that all these businesses have good reputations and the people we put through the lie detector tests all passed. The objects were and are still missing.

DUFFY

This is like the Bermuda triangle in Chicago. My problem is that no business seems safe from this scam. The mayor is on everyone's ass. The business people are pissed. The insurance companies are holding up payments because nothing makes sense. My squad is the joke around here, because movie, cartoon characters are the culprits. So, doctor maybe we do need a psychiatrist to help us. By the way doctor Why do you have an interest in weird crime cases? What makes you come to this particular police station and ask this type of question. Is there something you know about this type of scam or hoax?

DOCTOR

I do not know anything that might help you, yet. I will work on the problem and get back to you if I come up with anything.

The doctor is walking out of the precinct and he hears Rodrigues shout.

RODRIGUES

Hey Doc the hour is not up Duffy is still eating doughnuts and there is a PMS problem.

DOCTOR

I will be able to help you Rodrigues next time I am here. I will do your analysis for free.

The remarks by the doctor are followed by laughter as he walks out.

SCENE 4

This takes place in the FBI office in Chicago. The meeting is attended by a supervisor, a Virgil Ghlitly and two agents Zita Washington and Saul Levinson. Virgil is an elderly man, refined looking. He could be almost retired from his appearance. Zita is a middle aged black woman, very trim and well dressed, looks like a model, and Saul is an older man.

VIRGIL

Well we have another odd one to check out.

ZITA

You know Virgil . . . just one time I would like to investigate a normal crime. Give me a good old fashioned kidnapping, murder for hire across state lines, whatever.

VIRGIL

I know how you guys feel but because we are now completely integrated into the homeland security communications grid we have to play on a bigger team. We know that because of the terrorist attacks we have to be looking at all oddities, anomalies in behavior patterns. Years back if a guy in the suburbs bought a ton of fertilizer, no one cared to call the guy, and ask why he bought the fertilizer. Today, two or three agencies are alerted and must jump to see why the fertilizer was bought by a non farmer.

SAUL

So what is it today? A grand mother bought a lot of gunpowder and some fertilizer.

ZITA

Maybe someone took out some books from the library that are, on the no, no list,

VIRGIL?

Nothing, that simple for you today. It seems that two different cities are bothered by the same type of crime at the same time. This eliminates the possibility that the perpetrator is the same person. Chicago and Washington D.C. are the two cities where the same type of odd shit is happening.

ZITA

Ok, we are all ears.

VIRGIL

Well, I do not want you to laugh real laud, it makes the other people, outside this office, think we are telling jokes. Chicago is got a rash of burglaries that can not be explained. Somehow thieves enter locked stores, safes, and steal things without breaking windows, doors, walls, floors, or setting off the alarms on entering or leaving. When inside the premises they do set off motion alarms, and cameras. The police now come and find everything locked up tight, alarm still going inside. The owner or manager shows up they look at the triggered motion film and guess what they all see?

SAUL

Nothing?

ZITA

The little people, elves?

VIRGIL

Zita is right, almost.

Saul and Zita start laughing while Virgil motions with both hands to keep it down

VIRGIL

In Chicago, on the films, appear perpetrators wearing cartoon masks, like Porky Pig, plus Halloween masks, an Easter Bunny mask, and so on.

SAUL

No Batman bad guys, no super heroes show up? I am going to love this, I will tell my kids I am trying to catch the thieving Easter Bunny.

ZITA

I will tackle that nasty Porky Pig. Saul is Jewish he can not deal with pig criminals, it would not be Kosher. You are making this up Virgil, huh?

VIRGIL

I wish this was not real. I am mostly afraid that if this rash of crimes hits the news in the mass media, we will look like Elmer Fudd, protecting the carrot patch from that nasty wabbit. I could see the headlines now. Porky Pig the bandit outsmarts the FBI. FBI stumped by Easter Bunny. The papers are running some stories but not putting together a cartoon crime wave, yet, thank God.

ZITA

This is real?

VIRGIL

The Washington D.C. weird crime rash is dumber. Places are being robbed the same way. No sign of breaking or entering, inside alarms are set off, stuff is missing, and perpetrators are filmed. The good part for us is that they are not wearing masks and have been identified.

SAUL

So pick them up.

VIRGIL

No can do. They are paralyzed war veterans, there are two of them at Walter Reed hospital, they are confined in their beds. They are confined there and have never left their ward or the hospital. They are in rehab learning how to walk and move. They came in from Iraq, I guess almost dead and paralyzed.

ZITA

So they have twins.

VIRGIL

Nope, it is them, they left their fingerprints.

SAUL

So what do the cops say? How do they explain the two veterans appearing in the crime scenes?

VIRGIL

Most of the explanations vary but lean to the idea that the cameras are being tampered by someone with a sense of humor.

ZITA

So what is mostly missing?

VIRGIL

Missing are medications from locked, secure rooms in the hospital, money from local businesses. The area of activity seems to be spreading and the amounts of missing items are increasing in number and value. That is why this alert was triggered. A city by itself with a crime rash like this might not get attention. Two cities going through the same type of odd crime get attention. I want one of you to go to Washington and get all the information on this case. Talk to the FBI, and the detective in charge in Washington DC, and bring back everything they have on the case. Copies of everything, films, alarm records, fingerprint copies, crime scene photos, type of alarms, who maintains them, owners of stores. I also want the hospital security records. Interview the two veterans in the rehab, give them a polygraph test. The one that does the Chicago area, please do the same. Get me everything on this.

ZITA

If it is ok with Saul I would prefer to do Chicago.

SAUL

It is ok, I need some change anyway.

ZITA

Vigil, should I try to also polygraph Porky Pig and the Easter Bunny if they are caught?

VIRGIL

No, not by yourself. I would go out into the main office and ask for volunteers to help you polygraph the Pig and the Bunny. Please Zita, do not do that. Please be advised to keep this investigation to yourselves. We do not want to be known as the daring agents chasing cartoon characters.

ZITA

Mum is the word, right Saul?

VIRGIL

We meet again when Saul gets back. I want all the information or progress reports and I want answers, opinions in report form gleaned out from the materials you gathered. Understood . . . ? Good luck.

Meeting ends.

SCENE 5

This scene starts in a restaurant of the office building were Dr. Philip Fishbein has his practice. The Dr. is sitting at one of the tables and reading the paper. There is a cup of coffee in front of him. He has an appointment with Peter and his wife Janet. As the doctor sips his coffee he looks over the newspaper and sees Peter and a very good looking brunet walking up to his table. The woman is very well dressed and looks like she is about thirty years old.

DOCTOR

Well I see you made it, please join me.

PETER

Doctor Fishbein, this is my wife Janet.

DOCTOR

Janet, it is a pleasure to meet you.

JANET

Peter has been telling me all about you.

DOCTOR

Well I hope it is all good.

PETER

I told her that you do not believe me. Janet said that was ok. She did not believe me either, at first.

JANET

I was convinced he was crazy until he started coming back with all kinds of nice things.

PETER

That is the only way I can prove what has happened to me.

DOCTOR

You mean somehow stealing things? Is this how you will explain your condition, by robbing banks, and jewelry stores?

PETER

I want you to know, believe, that this is happening to me. I need a reality check from you, so I do not think I am living in a dream fantasy, or I am totally insane. I need you to explain what is happening to me.

DOCTOR

I want to help you. What you describe is impossible, yet you seem intent to prove it is possible. Your wife is now convinced you are doing the impossible. So now I have two patients all of a sudden.

JANET

Hold up there doctor, I am as sane as you.

DOCTOR

That is not saying a whole lot Janet. You see I went to talk to the police as Peter suggested. And guess what?

JANET

The cops think you are crazy?

DOCTOR

No, I just asked questions about odd cases. However Peter was right in that the cops have a whole squad assigned to investigate unexplained burglaries. There are even stories in the paper of strange robberies. The consensus in the police is that the images are computer generated and that this is more a scam type crime rather than a burglary

JANET

You did not tell them about Peter?

DOCTOR

No, it is a doctor, patient, privacy situation, and I did not say anything. However I think the police might get curious about a psychiatrist who is interested in something that is making them frustrated. Why in the world would a psychiatrist walk into that particular police station and ask specifically about some unexplained crimes. I think I set of some signals.

JANET

What if they question you?

DOCTOR

I will not say anything to the police, but I need to know from Peter how he got my book out of my office?

PETER

I told you what I can do. You also heard from the cops what I am capable of doing

DOCTOR

So if you convince me what you can do, what do you want me to do? Why are you here?

JANET

What we wanted to know from you is if this out of body travel is possible, have you heard of this before, also, a reality check mostly for my husband to convince him he is not insane.

DOCTOR

Let us say at some point Peter convinces me he can do this. I am saying this as mental masturbation, the what if game. Do you realize if this is real how big this is? Do you realize what the ramifications of this can be to you, to me, to the army, national defense? What will happen to all of our lives when different governments find this talent is available? You would be the most desired tool for any government and the most dangerous tool to all governments that do not have you.

PETER

My life would not be my own. None of our lives would be worth anything.

DOCTOR

I still think it is a scam or trick of some sort done with computers. I would however recommend to you to stop talking about it to anybody. I would also suggest if it is you, to please stop the scam and let this thing fade away. No detectives want to work on what they perceive as impossible cases. The paperwork will be filed away and forgotten. If you have any scammed merchandise, money, I would mail it back secretly.

JANET

No, why should we return something that only the insurance companies pay for. I say fuck the insurance companies as they fuck us. We had a life, we were well off and then after the accident the insurance refused certain treatment options, the small type on the back of the policy was outlining how to fuck us out of our savings. We still do not have health insurance because now we have a pre existing condition and no one wants to insure us. Why should we try to convince you at a hundred dollars an hour, per visit. You do not know how it feels to loose all you worked for. I also was forced by the hospital lawyers to give them all the money in a small trust fund I had from my grandparents. Your suggestion now is for us to become a homeless couple, start all over from zero. You have no idea how broke and in debt we were when Peter came out of the hospital. I say fuck the insurance companies. We are not returning anything.

PETER

I agree with Janet. If I was stealing from individuals, as an honest person, somewhat a Catholic, I could not do it.

Insurance companies are the biggest rip off artists in humankinds history. Look at the hurricane destroyed houses. People paid for the policies for decades and then the hurricane winds pushed the sea, the water, up to destroy the homes and the insurance said it was a flood and they were not covered. Why do we not ask the people who lost everything how to handle insurance companies?

DOCTOR

Hold up there, I do not get into moral arguments with my patients or their spouses.

PETER

Good, when I need moral guidance, feel guilty, I will go see my priest, Father Valentine O'Brien. All I want from you doctor is to explain my condition, tell me I am not dreaming or insane.

DOCTOR

I told you what I think. It is a trick, like a magic trick, done with the help of computers. Either you are lying to me or doing it subconsciously, or someone is using you as a prop in their scam.

JANET

I believe in what Peter can do. I have the money, jewelry, what can we do to show you this is real? Peter can travel out of body, he can also become physically present at an site. He can pick up physical objects and dematerialize from the site with them.

PETER

I did it with the book in your office.

JANET

Tell the good doctor of one of your earliest escapades. Your dream travel adventure that almost ended in divorce.

PETER

When I was a salesman on the road I would stop in sometimes in one of the strip places, and buy myself a lap dance. That is all it was, simple entertainment. You know those places doc.

DOCTOR

I certainly do not frequent those places.

PETER

Maybe as you say not frequently but only on occasion.

DOC

Please, is there a point somewhere in this conversation?

PETER

The point is that when I was still paralyzed I kept materializing in this one strip club. I believed at that time that these were just dreams of a sick frustrated man. I got to know a very beautiful, young, brunet striper, and after closing of the club I had sex with her many times.

DOCTOR

You must have dreamt it.

JANET

Suffice it to say he was fucking this bimbo every night while his body lay paralyzed in bed. I forgave him because he told me about the dreams. I believed at that time they were just what you call wet dreams because he could not masturbate at that time.

DOCTOR

So what is the point? It was a dream, yes, a wet dream. Very normal, Peter is however a little old to have wet dreams. Fantasies, yes.

JANET

The point is that this bimbo, called April, shows up at our house with a baby. Her real name is Ann Layghton. She meets me and Peter. Identifies Peter, and says she has no intention of breaking up our marriage, only needs a little help in taking care of the baby.

DOCTOR

How did she find Peter?

JANET

Peter the dream lover was not real bright. He had company paperwork in the car where he was playing hide the salami with this nineteen year old bimbo. She remembered the company name and they told her how to find Peter.

DOCTOR

I am curious why she did not opt for an abortion.

JANET

She explained it by the fact that her periods were not regular. She did not know she was pregnant until way into the pregnancy, besides she is catholic.

DOCTOR

So how did it end?

JANET

I told her to take her bullshit elsewhere. I said that Peter was paralyzed at the time she is accusing him of bonking her. She told me all she wanted was for Peter to get a DNA test. You know, who is the daddy type test. She said she had the baby DNA done and if Peter is not the daddy we would never see her again.

DOCTOR

So how did it end?

PETER

I am having a test done on my DNA. We are waiting for results. The baby boy looks like me.

JANET

Shut up Peter.

DOCTOR

Well Peter I feel this scam of yours is like a large snowball rolled in snow, getting bigger all the time, harder to push for the truth as its size increases.

PETER

I love Janet very much. I am confused about the baby, and what April claims as real.

DOCTOR

I think you should write a book on how to cheat on the spouses. Title could be, dream lovers.

JANET

You are not going to charge us for this meeting I hope?

DOCTOR

No, I do not think this is therapy, I should pay you, this is so confusing that it is becoming entertaining, and could I have April's number, no, I am joking.

PETER

You still think this is a scam?

DOCTOR

Does it not puzzle both of you that a sick, paralyzed man dreams himself into a healthy body, I say healthy enough to have sex with a nineteen year old stripper. His body is paralyzed, yet in his dream he is cured. Something is wrong in this equation, if it were real and not a dream. How do you become cured in you new body?

PETER

I have no idea. We are waiting for the DNA results. Can we see you when we get the results?

DOCTOR

Yes, absolutely yes. I also would like to contact Dr. Mustafa and see what kind of drugs he gave you to cause, possibly hallucinations.

PETER

I will try to locate him for you. We should have the DNA results next week. Can we meet in your office next Friday at nine in the morning.

They all get up to leave

DOCTOR

Yes, see you then.

All leave the restaurant.

SCENE 6

Levinson enters the FBI office in Washington D.C. He approaches the reception desk which is separated from the reception area by bullet proof glass. The most beautiful receptionist with very large boobs greets him and he announces he is here to see agent Kuster. Levinson now sits down and is waiting. Moments later a metal door opens and in steps a stocky, round faced, blond haired man. As Levinson stands up he says.

LEVINSON

Agent Kuster I presume?

KUSTER

Yes, and you are Levinson, the Levinson I heard about, from the Chicago office?

LEVINSON

The same, you have heard of me? I was involved in that big bust of the Arian Brotherhood. They had bought 5 tons of fertilizer.

KUSTER

Interesting story how today the sales of fertilizer raises the danger flags. But tell me why in the world has Virgil decided to send you here in person? We could just as well have sent all the information to you.

LEVINSON

I think it was done out of frustration in our team. We had run into a brick wall of so called evidence. The clues led to impossible possibilities, fantasies. Our only explanation was a computer scam of some sort which we had our computer geeks working on.

KUSTER

Well, at least we have all that in common with your office.

LEVINSON

Kuster, are you related in any way to the last stand guy in the Little Big Horn fame.

KUSTER

No I am Polish, my real name was Kusterowsky and that would have had a tongue twisting affect on most Americans.

LEWINSON

So all we have is a total of nothing between two FBI offices.

KUSTER

Well, maybe a little more than just nothing or maybe just a bigger nothing. We ran a lot of tests on the two paralyzed vets and saw something that made us start considering some impossible scenarios.

LEVINSON

From weird to weirder.

KUSTER

There is a new MRI machine we used on the two vets. This is a new machine that is the first to follow the flow of sodium, allowing it to see the firing of individual brain cells instantaneously. The results were astounding. The brains of normal people were like night and day compared to the vet brains. Their brains had no unused sections, the sleep centers were connected to all other functions of the brain.

LEVINSON

This is all very interesting except for the fact that you had them on camera and their finger prints, and you found evidence in their rooms. They are the perpetrators it would seem to me.

KUSTER

Very true except they are paralyzed and can not walk.

LEVINSON

So they are lying.

KUSTER

We ran every kind of test on their legs, they can not walk, yet. They are improving from an illegal stem cell drug regimen given to them by a doctor Mustafa. The drugs are a concoction of stem cell derivatives. We are sure they will be able to walk soon, but not right now. The good doctor Mustafa has also now disappeared.

LEVINSON

What do the vets say?

KUSTER

They laugh at you, and claim they are being set up by the tooth fairy or some other type of goblin. We also noticed an increase of arrogance and aggression when we talked to them. It is strange when it comes from people that can not piss by themselves.

LEVINSON

So you ran all the tests, and the results could not be interpreted in a normal way?

KUSTER

The polygraph was inconclusive, as if all the answers pertaining to the burglaries were true and false at the same time.

LEVINSON

So the biggest task forces, biggest budgets, latest spy techniques can not explain how cartoon characters in Chicago rob places and how the same type of robberies are perpetrated in our capitol.

KUSTER

We have not given up. When we concluded that it was possibly a computer scam we put on our best geeks on it. They got no answers so we went into another area and this was the area of paranormal phenomenon.

LEVINSON

I knew all the jokes in Chicago had a sound basis. It is the tooth fairy and Porky Pig.

KUSTER

Well we are not laughing and we invited several experts in the paranormal area to look into this. We have a professor Tony Abbot helping us, he works with the Journal of Parapsychology. He deals in psychic phenomena like telepathy, extra-sensory perception, psychokinesis and post-mortem survival studies like reincarnation, ghosts, and hauntings.

LEVINSON

It is hard to believe I am hearing this kind of shit in a Washington FBI office. Maybe we all need brain scans?

KUSTER

Come up with a better idea to follow and you will get a big promotion, I am sure. You may not be aware that our little investigation into this weirdness has attracted some top people in the defense department and army intelligence, and the White house.

LEVINSON

I knew that the army was very interested in the possibility of telepathy and telekinesis for waging war and spying.

KUSTER

Well they had some success with their experiments and when they heard about our weird cases they offered to help. They also did not want their involvement to attract any attention. I think they feel if there is, something, in these strange cases then secrecy is very important.

LEVINSON

So what now? I will call my office and tell Virgil about the status here.

KUSTER

Why don't you wait till after we meet with professor Abbot at two this afternoon, and see what he says, and then call Virgil.

LEVINSON

I will do that. I will see you at two.

Both men stand up shake hands and as Levinson walks out he looks at the receptionist who is standing and clearing something off her desk, she bends over to pick something up and her boobs are displayed. Levinson trips on the carpeting while staring at her. He stumbles, but catches his balance. Kuster laughs.

SCENE 7

One of the larger conference rooms in the FBI offices. Levinson is in attendance, Kuster is in charge of meeting, two army officers with a lot of decorations, two men in dark suits, a woman that looks like Vampirela, and a little old man with long white hair, who looks like Joda, from Star Wars. There is also a very tall well dressed black man, detective Sam White, from DC.

KUSTER

Please take your seats we will start the meeting (everyone takes a seat) My name is Kuster, agent in charge of the present problem, and I am responsible for bringing you all here to the FBI offices to try and clear this problem up my memos to the Homeland security triggered an alert with all of you. Let me introduce all of you. The two army officers are colonel Roberts, and colonel Gerhardt from army intelligence. We also have a representative from Homeland security, Mr Chester Kyber, and the defense department is represented by Mr Arv Tamul. We also have detective Sam White from D.C. who has been working on this problem. And from the windy city Chicago, we have FBI agent, Levinson. Today I invited two guests, to present to us some different views of looking at this particular problem, they are professor Tony Abbot and Ms. Rita Lenska. I will let them tell you about themselves and their field of study. Professor if you will start out please.

ABBOT

I feel very strange being here before you. All my life I dealt with the paranormal studies and here I am talking to you, who are dealing constantly with logical realities. This is like oil and water, they do not mix. Reason, logic, and our human senses are impossible to integrate, or use, into analyzing the paranormal or even explaining basic world religions. I am here to simply tell you what has been done in the paranormal areas, you draw you own conclusions

KUSTER

I would like to clarify that the reason we reached out to Professor Abbot was that we ran out of logical explanations. The computer scam theory of ours did not pan out and we were left with no theories. There were no answers to what we saw on the tapes.

ABBOT

When logic, reason, and the reality of our senses are not present man is left to his fantasies, imagination, that is the basis of all religions and the paranormal quests. When the possible is peeled away like an onion and you are left with nothing, man begins to look at the nothing. Mankind can not accept an unknown nothing as an answer. Sometimes pure fantasy replaces the unknown nothing. Today modern man, reasoning man, can not accept explanations based on imagination and fantasy so we evolve into the study of paranormal trying to apply our scientific methods to this study. This is an attempt to explain the unexplainable. This is why we are here today. Agent Kuster can give you a little more detail.

KUSTER

I think you all read my reports on the mini crime spree here at Walter Reed and the D.C. area. The seeming perpetrators are photographed at the crime scene and are also locked up and under camera surveillance in their ward, in the hospital, at the same time. Their fingerprints are at the crime scene. Stolen stuff is found in their rooms, yet they are just barely able to move. The illegal stem cell drugs, given to them by this Doctor Mustafa are slowly restoring movement in their lower extremities. Detective White can tell you a little more about this.

WHITE

Well agent Kuster gave you a very good description of the situation. We saw these two paralyzed veterans on film, actually running around, laughing, as if they had no paralysis at all. Yet when we checked them out in the hospital, the medical opinion was that the film and the people in bed can not be the same. Fingerprints are also unexplainable. It is their fingerprints at the crime sites. Polygraph tests are also inconclusive. I guess that is why we are all here.

COLONEL GERHARDT

That is exactly why we are here. We feel that it is imperative to solve this phenomenon, especially since Chicago also broke out in the same kind of crime rash. We feel that if the smallest possibility exists that this type of crime can occur as we see it, then it presents to all of us the worst nightmare scenario. Imagine foreign spies appearing, disappearing, in our most secret project sites. Imagine the perpetrator in Chicago, who appears sometimes as Porky Pig, appearing in Fort Knox and disappearing with a bar of gold.

KUSTER

Well let us let the professor continue.

ABBOT

Where was I? O, I was trying to explain the unexplainable. (He laughs here) Well anyway, while science, today, is explaining a lot of the mysteries that were deemed as magical, or miracles in the old days, we in the paranormal studies have also advanced some new theories. Our latest and most promising study pertains to the Leibnitz monad theory. This is a particle theory, that all matter in the universe is made up of small particles called monads by Leibnitz. Yesterday we called it an atom and today we go to a smaller particle which we now call a Higgs—Bosun particle. This, today is believed to be the God particle, the absolutely basic building block of all forms in the universe. So in the span of four hundred years from the theory of Leibnitz and his monad we are breaking down the atom and its parts to the God Particle and proving that what Leibnitz postulated so long ago is true.

KUSTER

Professor I think you lost most of us here. What does this monad have to do with us?

ABBOT

I am getting to that. The so called God particles give all things their substance and shape, they are the basic building blocks of all existing things, just as monads in Leibnitz world give everything their form and makeup.

KUSTER

So what you are suggesting is a science fiction idea of a shape shifting possibility, the so called monads or God Particles changing forms. Is this where we are going with your presentation?

ABBOT

In a way, yes. However in the context of our paranormal theory we advance that the reformulation of the God particle to different forms can be done by some individuals at their will. We are in the process right now of doing some experiments. I would like at this time to let Rita tell you a little bit about her world wide group of people who are researching the so called occult. They are gathering data on shape shifting legends such as our American Indians talk about, to the vampires in the European legends. Rita tell us about you research, please.

RITA

Well I will do my best telling you my side of the story. I am not used to speak to skeptics, which I am sure you all are. Vampires, shape shifters, ghosts are not easy to discuss in a society that depends on science, logic, and reality. Religion today is the last bastion not based on the principle of logic and reason. Most of old time magic has been eliminated by the scientific methods. That is why today it is difficult to present miracles as was done in the old days. A good example is that exorcism is even frowned upon by the church.

Colonel Gerhardt raises his hand as if to speak and Rita motions for him to go ahead.

GERHARDT

Rita I am just curious why you dress like Vampirela and speak of research. Why do research when faith should be enough for you adherents.

RITA

I dress like Vampirela because it allows me into the very inner circles of the occult. If I told the villagers in let us say Romania that I had a PHD in Psych., they would not be as open, I tell them that we have an off beat interest in vampire stories and they open up. No one wants to feel like a bug under a microscope. This outfit allows me to get into witches covens and devil worshippers groups.

GERHARDT

But the whole concept of ghost, vampires, and such is based on faith in those things and magic or superstitions.

RITA

True enough in the past, that was enough to create believers in all those things. Today however, even the true believers have been also tainted by logic and reality. Reason is being applied today to explain the occult. Because of this, much of the old beliefs are disappearing. The churches are also experiencing the attack of reason. Faith is evolving into a more believable scenario.

GERHARDT

I take it you have no religion.

RITA

You must be psychic. (she laughs) I am an agnostic, that is the closest position that logic, and reason allows man to explain God. You colonel also must have some true religion I am sure backed up by tons of your own logic. I am also sure you are the type to try and spread your own logic to everyone.

Professor Abbot jumps up and says.

ABBOT

P lease, let us get on with the presentation. Rita, Please.

RITA

Sorry professor. As I was saying reason and reality are invading the paranormal areas. Houdini was one the greatest debunkers of the spiritualists. He exposed them, all the time, and showed that the contacts with the spirit world were faked. However at about the same time a man by the name of Charles Fort, collected about 40,000 paranormal notes. That many notes, we believe, can not all be false.

GERHARDT

Let me just remind you Miss. Rita that when Elvis Presley died, I believe 100,000 people claim they saw him, and are we to believe that because so many saw him, some did really see him? Numbers could be misleading.

RITA

Well I do not know how to answer that argument except to say that after Christ died only forty witnesses saw him when he rose from the dead, and that was enough to create a religion that has gone on for two thousand years, and in that time had billions of believers in what the forty witnesses saw. My point is that we must explore all accounts.

GERHARDT

Good answer Rita, please go on.

RITA

My research into the paranormal has taken me to many areas. I think the most physical evidence of weird, not normal happenings, are the perfectly preserved bodies of so called saints. There is no explanation of this in the scientific circles. The legends about these saints are many. They appear, disappear, work miracles and on and on.

KIUSTER

You also mentioned that there are less and less of these miracles, or magic today.

RITA

I did say that and we all know that to be true. Vampires, zombies, ghosts, miracles all fade before scientific scrutiny. Our group's contention is that all these things had some basis of truth at some point.

KUSTER

We are here today to explore some of the capabilities of these fantasy creatures. We want to hear about that.

RITA

Ok. Vampires have the ability, it is said, to change shape. They can appear as dogs, bats, fog, they can also move from one place to another at will. They need blood and can not be in the sun. They also have to sleep on their homeland dirt during the day. The bottom line to all these creatures that can teleport, do telekinesis and so forth all have a weakness built in that can destroy them.

KUSTER

So what you say is that if we have a shape shifter, a demon of sorts, we can defeat him because historically they all had a weakness.

RITA

Every dragon, demon or hero always had a weakness. All we have to do is figure out how these apparitions function and we will have a way to stop them

KUSTER

So the bottom line is that we know weird crimes, scams have happened in D.C. and Chicago, but we do not know how. We also know that the two paralyzed vets in Walter Reed are somehow involved. How about Chicago agent Levinson, what have you got on Porky Pig.?

LEVINSON

Nothing yet on the Pig, but we have been working closely with Chicago police and a detective Duffy has reported that a psychiatrist by the name of Fishbein had come into their offices and asked if there were any weird crimes occurring in Chicago. This was a red flag for all of us. Why would a very successful, respected doctor, come into a police station and ask this? We are now following up on this doctor looking for a connection.

KUSTER

We are looking at all the medical records of the two vets. I also believe that army intelligence will now question the vets and have a surveillance placed on them for all twenty four hours. So if there are no more questions, comments, we will meet again as soon as we have more data on this. Thank you all.

The group begins to disperse.

SCENE 8

This takes place outside the cashier's room at the race track. There are two guards at the door on the outside of this room. Regular activity in the hallway is taking place of people going about their business. The room across the hall from the cashier's room is the video surveillance and security room. Big glass window shows many monitor screens and two guards observing activities on the screens. Suddenly on one of the screens showing the inside of the cashier's room appears a person with a Porky Pig mask and begins to stuff the money on the table into a large duffle bag. The money is tied in large bundles and neatly stacked on the table. The guards in the surveillance room start the alarm procedures. Bells, lights, sirens go off.

FIRST GUARD IN SURVEILLANCE ROOM
Someone is in the Cashier's room.

SECOND GUARD IN SURVEILLANCE ROOM
Impossible, there are two guards outside the only door, look. (He points)

FIRST GUARD IN SURVEILLANCE ROOM
But look at the screen that is the cashier's room.

SECOND GUARD IN SURVEILLANCE ROOM
We need the manager with the second key to open the door. (He runs out holding a key)

Jerry the manager is running toward the cahier's room with the key out on a chain. The hall way is filled with ringing bells, sirens, and flashing lights. The surveillance guard with the second key meets him at the door. The two hallway guards have their guns pulled out. The door is opened with both keys and everyone rushes in. Porky Pig is holding the bag of money and is looking at everyone.

JERRY
Hold it right there Pig man, how did you get into this room?

PORKY PIG
I am not armed I do not want to hurt anyone. I just want to leave.

GUARD ONE
Are you fucking nuts, asshole? Put down the bag slowly and get your hands up.

PORKY PIG

I am sorry to upset all of you, the insurance will cover your money loses and I must leave right now.

GUARD ONE

You are nuts, drop the bag, pig man.

As the guard motions with his gun to set the bag down, Porky pig starts to disappear with the bag of money. Porky is gone. Jerry and the three guards are standing completely perplexed. The fourth guard rushes in and says.

FOURTH GUARD FROM SURVEILLANCE ROOM

My screen just showed Porky Pig vanish right from in front of you. What happened?

JERRY

That is just what happened, he disappeared and we look like idiots. I hope this shit is on the tapes from the screens, because no one will believe what we saw.

FIRST GUARD

I was here and I do not believe what I saw. The fuck just disappeared. I am glad there were five of us, the cops will have to believe us.

JERRY

I do not know if anyone will believe us, I do not believe what I saw. I think we all are going to have a problem.

SCENE 9

This takes place in Walter Reed hospital. We see two highly decorated soldiers walking down the corridor looking at room numbers. They stop by one door and one of them motions that this is the door. They enter into a room where there are two patients in their propped up beds watching television.

FIRST SOLDIER

Hi guys, you are Sergio Sanches and David Repsy I presume. My name is Major Al Glavin and this is Colonel Keith Larmon.

SERGIO

Hey mon we are so glad you are here mon. You gona get us one of the large plasma screen TV mon. We requested that a while back. Did you bring it?

GLAVIN

No, we do not know about any TV, but you already have a TV.

SERGIO

Mon, we want a bigger screen.

GLAVIN

Never mind the TV, we stopped by to ask some questions.

SERGIO

So ask away mon, and then get us the big TV.

GLAVIN

You guys talked to the police and FBI. You took some tests and all the investigating ended up creating more confusion. We want to know how some stolen property ended up in your room? We want to know how your fingerprints ended up in some of the rooms were stuff was pilfered?

DAVID

Why are you bothering us, you know we can not walk, we are paralyzed?

COLONEL LARMON

Lets cut the shit out, you know stolen stuff was in your room, you know you left fingerprints. You are now dealing with army intelligence, that's us. So please, no bullshit mon.

DAVID

Someone must have put the shit in our room and found a way to pick up our fingerprints from some object and leave them in those places. That is possible, is it not?

GLAVIN

Except you were also filmed, and identified in those places, and that is you guys even giving the cameras your finger.

SERGIO

Hey mon, we are paralyzed. We will ring for the nurse mon, if you keep annoying us.

GLAVIN

We do not want to annoy you. All we want to know is how you did all that?

DAVID

We are paralyzed man, we were almost killed in your stupid useless war, we can not use our legs, and you think we are running around stealing shit and giving people the finger.

COLONEL LARMON

You guys are not very patriotic when you are calling the war useless. You must understand that we are fighting for peace and freedom for America. You understand that, do you not?

SERGIO

Thank you for telling us mon. When we were picking up the bodies from bombed out houses, of women and little children, we did not realize this was a fight for peace and freedom.

GLAVIN

We did not come to talk about the war. All we want is some answers.

DAVID

We would like answers also, why we had to go kill Arabs for no reason. We would also like to know why we could not get experimental stem cell drugs in the US. Our good doctor Mustafa had to smuggle them in to test on us. The doctor told us that these illegal drugs might help repair our severed nerves. Obviously these drugs do not work on paralyzed soldiers, if they did, they would, of coarse be given to us by our loving government.

COLONEL LARMON

This country considers stem cell drugs or experiments with stem cells, a sin against God, and has banned them.

DAVID

To go to a useless war, kill innocent people, is that not a sin? To have thousands of American soldiers killed and maimed for no good reason is not a sin? To attempt to cure them with stem cell drugs is a sin. Are you so fucked up that you do not see how fucked up this country is where it involves morals or ethics? Where has logic and reason gone? Where have our principles gone on which this nation was founded? Why talk about stem cell sin when we supposedly have separation of church and state? Do you ever question how a nation deems something sinful when it should have no religious connections in it?

COLONEL LARMON

I did not know you were a philosopher.

DAVID

I am not a philosopher. I am only a person that thinks, reasons. There is not much else to do as I lay here in my shitted up diaper. You should try thinking Colonel and you do not have to shit in you pants to do it.

SERGIO

Hey David ask the Colonel to change you diaper, mon, and wash your ass.

DAVID

Yes Colonel we have to stay in our shitty diapers longer because of the cut backs in the budget. You see we have spent three trillion dollars on the needless war in Iraq and we are spending two billion per week in the useless war in Afghanistan, and we do not have any dollars left to hire an extra nurse or helper on our floor to help our wounded heroes from your war

SERGIO

Hey David where is your patriotism, just stay in your shit and be glad there is money for diapers.

GLAVIN

You guys are still in the army and subject to its rules. So stop the bitching and bullshiting.

DAVID

Our bullshit is miniscule if that is what you think it is. You two with your army are drowning in an ocean of bullshit. You were in a civil war in Iraq fighting both sides and also killing their people and ours and wasting billions of dollars for no reason. Now that is Bullshit.

GLAVIN

You are not going to help us get answers I guess?

SERGIO

Maybe mon, if you get us a big TV, I help you.

COLONEL HARMON

We could transfer you to high security area and make things worse if you do not cooperate.

SERGIO

Hey David be nice mon, they can send us to one of them countries were they can torture us.

DAVID

Sergio all they have to do is take away your diaper to torture you.

SERGIO

Mon I had enough of this shit, I ring for the nurse.

He rings for the nurse and in a little while a black nurse walks in with a file in her hand.

DAVID

Nurse these two guys are leaving I hope, they are stressing us out.

NURSE

Visiting hours ended a while back, we have to change their diapers and feed them. Here is the file on their progress, I believe they are improving.

COLONEL LARMON

You guys think this is a joke or a debate, just know that we will be back and we will get answers to our questions.

DAVID

I told you Sergio they have ways to make you talk and like Arnold says "I will be Back".

The two officers leave.

SCENE 10

This takes place in the Pentagon. Top secret conference room. Two MP's outside door. Five men are inside sitting around the conference table. An older general, Gint Soltis and on one side are the two colonels, Jim Roberts and Steve Gerhardt. The colonels are the ones that were at the meeting with professor Abbot and Rita Lenska. On the other side sit Major Al Glavin and Colonel Keith Larmon who met with the sick vets.

GENERAL GINT

Well here we are. My top stars in my army intelligence unit and me sitting with a file full of unbelievable bullshit. We could have coffee, talk sports, and go for a beer and shit can the file. But unfortunately for all of us I have a meeting with the president who got curious about the events and wants some answers tomorrow. Weeell someone please shed some light on this file.

JIM ROBERTS

We were at a meeting with Homeland, FBI, Washington Police, Paranormal experts and gave you the info in the file.

KEITH LARMON

We also gave you the report on the two vets involved in this situation.

GENERAL GINT

The sum total of what all of you gave me is what I call bullshit.

JIM ROBERTS

With due respect general . . . we gave you what we got from the meetings. We gave you facts. If you choose to see them as bullshit that is your choice.

GENERAL GINT

I do not mean to insult you, but what I expected from all of you is to look beyond what is presented and debunk the bullshit. I do not accept paranormal events, I do not accept miracles, vampires, shape shifters. I will not go to the president and tell him that a guy that looks like Porky Pig robs banks and vanishes. I expect you to figure out how this scam works, who works it. I will put off the president for a week by telling him we are gathering data from all agencies. I will have reasonable answers from all of you or you will be on patrol duty in a weather station in the South Pole.

JIM ROBERTS

General we tried to debunk already by asking the computer geeks and security camera people for answers. There are so far no answers and not even good theories.

GENERAL GINT

I worked with you guys for several years. You know I am not a difficult person to work with. Let me explain why this stupid situation is important to solve. This phenomena or as I believe scam has potential to upset a lot of agencies, a lot of people.

What I am saying it has potential to create panic. An example would be to have, this character Porky Pig, appear in the Pentagon. Another example would be to have the two paralyzed vets appear in some embassy or the White House. Panic of unbelievable proportions would be created.

JIM ROBERTS

We fully understand the panic factor. What is in back of our minds is that if this is not a computer scam, if it is real, it will create a tsunami in all diplomatic and political interactions. The relations of nations, agencies, corporations will be turned upside down. Our world as we know will have to be rebuilt completely if the phenomena is possible and real.

GENERAL GINT

Thank you for you assessment Jim. I give your assessment one percent odds that this is a working phenomena. How ever the results would be so devastating that I have to consider solutions if this is real.

JIM ROBERTS

If we get any concrete proof that this theory of Professor Abbot, of the so called God Particles shifting to different forms at will, we will have to have a plan to isolate everyone that can know how it works or work it.

GENERAL GINT

Isolation is a mild word for this phenomena. The knowledge of it would have to be suppressed, erased. Just imagine if China or Russia had Porky Pig working for them.

JIM ROBERTS

Our plan to get more facts on this is to question a psychiatrist in Chicago who has drawn attention from the FBI and police in Chicago. It seems a Dr. Fishbein walked into a Chicago precinct where Porky Pig has been popping up and asked if there were any weird unsolvable crimes committed. The precinct was plagued by weird robberies and had set up a special squad to look into these events. When Fishbein asked about weird events all kinds of flags went up.

GENERAL GINT

That seems like a connection. You have to go and get answers. At this stage I believe the approach is still gentle. If the odds of one percent change I give you full authority to use whatever means you have to use to get answers. Also if our two suspect vets appear anywhere else put them immediately in isolation wards, separate them and put a twenty four hour guards to watch them Lets get some answers and good luck.

Meeting ends.

SCENE 11

The office reception area of Dr. Philip Fishbein. A nice little old lady receptionist looks up and sees two military men walk in.

RECEPTIONIST

Can I help you gentlemen?

FIRST MILITARY MAN.

We would like to see Dr. Fishbein. I am colonel Jim Roberts and this is colonel Keith Larmon.

RECEPTIONIST

You do not have an appointment and his next patient is due in at any minute.

KEITH LARMON

We will not take long and we have to fly back to Washington this evening.

RECEPTIONIST

I will ask him if he will see you.(She buzzes the Dr. and gets up to lead them into his office)

DR. FISHBEIN

Gentlemen what do I owe this visit to. One of you sick or . . . or.

JIM ROBERTS

Dr. my name is colonel Jim Roberts and this is colonel Keith Larmon. We are here from army intelligence department. We would like to ask you a few questions.

DR. FISHBEIN

I was also curious about army intelligence, I might also ask you some questions.

JIM ROBERTS

I will cut right to the chase Doctor. Why did you go to a Chicago police station and ask about weird crimes in their area? What would prompt a very highly regarded psychiatrist go to a particular precinct, not in his area, and ask such a question?

DR. FISHBEIN

I was simply curious about odd crimes and criminals. My work is in dealing with abnormal behavior patterns.

KEITH LARMON

You have to admit Doctor that the coincidence of that precinct being plagued by odd crimes and you showing up to find out about odd crimes does not fit well in our mind as simple chance coincidence.

DR. FISHBEIN

I do not see why I should be concerned about your perception of events.

KEITH LARMON

Your perception of why we are here asking this question is invalid because you do not realize that the police departments in two cities, the FBI in two cities, Homeland Security, the Defense Department and army intelligence are all interested in talking to you. Under the Patriot Act we can put a lot of pressure to get answers. You can simplify everything by telling us what you know. We will file a report to everyone concerned and no one will bother you

DR. FISHBEIN

You must realize that I have certain patient Doctor rules about divulging information.

KEITH LARMON

Let me put it this way Doctor. Your rules are trumped by national security and the defense department.

DR. FISHBEIN

You are in some way here threatening and intimidating me. I can get sued by my patients if I break the patient Doctor privileges. I think I will have to ask you to leave and contact me through my lawyer. Receptionist will give you his number.

KEITH LARMON

You managed a stall dear Doctor. Maybe you can just answer a generic question? Is there some unexplained phenomena you are concerned with in your practice?

DR. FISHBEIN

Yes.

KEITH LARMON

We will set up a meeting with all concerned and your lawyer.

The colonels leave and the Doctor scratches his head.

SCENE 12

Dr. Fishbein rings the doorbell of Peter Metcalf's house and the door opens and Peter is surprised to see the Doctor.

PETER

A real surprise Doctor. A house call by my psychiatrist.

DOCTOR

Lot of surprises Peter. I think we better get honest with each other. You will not believe as to who is interested in your hallucinations.

PETER

Ok, who can possibly know aside from you and Janet about my condition.?

DOCTOR

Try the army intelligence, homeland security, Chicago police

PETER

How could they know about me?

DOCTOR

They do not know about you. They only know that weird crimes are taking place in Chicago and Washington D.C. They also know that I am involved with these weird crimes.

PETER

You? How you?

DOCTOR

When you told me about some of the things you did I went to area precinct 31, and asked if there is some weird plague of crimes. Guess what? Yes there is a lot going on and they have a special squad under a detective Duffy investing the weird stuff. The squad at this point is a mod squad like group that is looked at more like a joke.

PETER

Jesus Christ, why did you do it? Go there, I mean.

DOCTOR

I wanted to verify what you said you are able to do.

PETER

Who questioned you?

DOCTOR

Two colonels from army intelligence claiming that homeland security, defense department, FBI are all interested in this phenomenan.

PETER

What did you tell them about me?

DOCTOR

I used the patient doctor privilege and put them off. This is only temporary because they want to see me again with my lawyer, and I am sure they will bring in their big guns.

PETER

Jesus, what the hell can I do?

DOCTOR

I think you have two options. Return all the stolen stuff and plea bargain, or do what you do best and disappear.

Meanwhile Janet walks into the room and says.

JANET

I heard the last part and the first option is off the table because we spent a lot of the cash and can not return it. Also I will not accept my husband going to jail.

DOCTOR

I think this is much bigger than anyone of us thought. You have to understand that if we accept the premise that Peter can travel out of body, and do things, he will be grabbed up by the military as a super secret all powerful weapon. All of our lives will not be our own.

PETER

I think no matter how you slice it I am in deep shit.

DOCTOR

I think that can be said for all of us. If your talents are real I think all of us will be deemed as top national secrets. The question will only be how deep the secret knowledge will be buried.

PETER

What will you do?

DOCTOR

I will meet with the big guns, the lawyers and try to stall. I feel if this is real it is bigger than any tsunami in human history. I would recommend you get a rented car from someone, pack your stuff and throw a dart at a US map and go there. I will meet with the big guns and have a plane ticket to some far off land and leave the same day after meeting before they pull my pass port.

PETER

You think it is that bad?

DOCTOR

As I am beginning to believe you can do what you have been telling me, it begins to dawn on me that your type of power is unacceptable in our world today. The consequences for nations having people like you working for them, is impossible to comprehend.

JANET

On top of all this shit, Peter has a conscience problem on what he has done with April. This was aggravated by the DNA test that came in showing Peter as the daddy of that slut's baby.

PETER

Janet please, let us put this behind us. We gave April enough money to raise and educate the boy.

DOCTOR

I think we should all step of this coming train wreck if the phenomenon is real. All of us should disappear.

JANET

We have not told you, but Peter also contacted doctor Mustafa to get some answers about his condition. There is a meeting set up, but we will not tell you where or when.

DOCTOR

You know Janet after I find myself in the middle of a swamp that I put myself in, I do not want to go deeper into it by knowing anything more. I would recommend you ask this doctor Mustafa how to stop this phenomenon.

PETER

I am so confused as to what to do. I think I need Father Valentine O'Brian who in the past has guided me. I, long ago was a practicing Catholic but then became an agnostic. Today my life is becoming a bit of a bad dream. I thought my problems are over with because we have all the money we need, and then you tell me all this new shit.

DOCTOR

Why not take this one step at a time. I will contact you on your cell phone number after my meeting with the colonels.

JANET

We will be on our way somewhere when you call us.

DOCTOR

I tried to help you. You know that.

PETER

I know, good by Doctor.

Doctor leaves.

SCENE 13

This is a conference room in Chicago Police Precinct 31. Attending meeting are the Duffy squad members: Maurice Ward and Ann Bic and detective Duffy. Sitting at head of table is Captain Vito Simagalia.

VITO

Do you guys know why I called this meeting?

Silence only can be heard

ANN

We are getting commendations and promotions, maybe?

VITO

You always have a sense of humor . . . not that I do not appreciate it sometimes. This time I have aaaa biiig problem and I do not want to have it by myself I want to share it with you.

DUFFY

Is it something we did?

VITO

No it happens this time it is something your mod squad did not do. You have not solved one tiny part of these weird robberies and guess what?

MAURICE

Ok, ok, what?

VITO

I put your squad on an easy, goofy, problem, hoping you can work together, learn procedures, methods, and do no harm to our precinct. However, I never in my wildest dreams thought anyone would be interested in your work, but, guess what?

DUFFY

You are beating around the bush . . . please captain.

VITO

My problem has become your problem because now everybody in this country is interested in your weird cases. For starters, army intelligence, FBI, the defense department, homeland security, are all interested in your work. My little ass is now called to explain everything to all theeese fucking people. The patriot act is bopped on my head to open all my files, and guess what? All my files are filled with your bullshit or nothing I can give these people to get them of my back.

Duffy

Captain that is what we got from all these cases. We tried working different theories such as computer scams, security camera manipulation, insider crime, and nothing made sense.

Vito

Washington D.C. has the same rash of crimes committed at the same time, so it can not be the same people.

Duffy

So what do you want us to do?

Vito

I want you to get me something real for my fucking files. Go out, all of you to the ripped off race track and file a complete report on this supposed robbery by disappearing Porky Pig. Please get some real answers. I can not talk to all the government agencies about bullshit and show them empty files.

Duffy

We are on it captain. We will not let you down.

The officers leave the room and Vito sits there holding his head, face with both hands as telephones ring all over.

SCENE 14

The race track meeting room. While waiting for the security guards to arrive the mod squad consisting of Maurice Ward, Ann Bic, and Duffy sit and talk among themselves.

DUFFY

Well guys . . . what the fuck are we going to give the captain?

ANN

I know we are going to get here the some dead end bullshit as in all the other cases.

MAURICE

Ann is right.

DUFFY

Well I invited the top geek, a computer hacker, security camera manipulator to take apart that cash counting room. I want him to pull out all the plugs, check out each wire, check each camera, check out each inch of film and tell me how this shit was done.

ANN

Who is this guy?

DUFFY

An old friend of mine. I arrested him a few times but he helped me out in some computer crime cases and I helped him with the judges and we became sort of friends.
His name is well known in the underground businesses, he goes by Tony, the weasel, Elbin.

The door opens and five men walk in. Introductions start.

DUFFY

I am detective Duffy, these are my associates Ann Bic, Maurice ward.

JERRY

I am Jerry Kay the head cashier these are the security guards. Ron, James, Peter and Paul. Sound like the apostles . . . huh?

DUFFY

Sorry for not laughing Jerry. Our squad is in deep shit with a ton of higher ups who want answers. We read the reports and get nothing about this case that makes sense.

JERRY

Let me allow Peter to give you a step by step occurrence of this million dollar robbery. Peter.

PETER

Well Ron and I are standing outside the cash counting, storage room. The room has bullet proof glass and steel frame doors with double locks. It takes two keys from two people to get in. I have one key and Jerry has the other one. We are not looking in the room, just talking, when from across the hall comes running James yelling at us that someone is in the room. By this time the bells are ringing and sirens going off. We look through the window and sure enough there is an asshole in the room with a Porky Pig mask stuffing money in a duffle bag. We see Jerry running toward us with the second key in his hand. I reach for my key on a chain and insert it in my lower lock. The Pig looks at us and finishes stuffing the money, zips the bag shut. I smile, I know the Pig has no escape, he does not hold a gun, all we have to do is go in and get him. Jerry sticks his key in and we push the door open. The confrontation with the pig is in the files as to what was said. The Pig just tells us he wants to leave and is not armed. We all think this is funny, I tell the Pig to drop the bag and he simply vanishes in front of all four of us. Now Paul comes running out of the surveillance monitor room and yells at us that Porky Pig just vanished from his screen.

DUFFY

Thank you Peter for a nice presentation of what you think you all saw. Now I will have, with your permission Jerry one of my computer geeks go over your computers, your wiring and your cameras. Is that OK?

JERRY

Please do. I will ask our general manager if we can reinvestigate again.

DUFFY

If you only knew how much pressure is on me to get answers.

JERRY

We are having a big problem with the bonding company and insurance carriers, and so please do what the hell you have to figure this shit out.

The guards leave and Duffy turns to Ann and Maurice.

DUFFY

Well there is your report from the witnesses. Now it is up to Tony to give us something.

MAURICE

Could this be an inside scam by the four guards and Jerry?

ANN

You looked at the reports. All five of them passed the polygraph test perfectly. If there were lies involved one of them would have stumbled on something.

DUFFY

Ok, so they did not do it. Someone did. Someone, somehow, scammed the surveillance and stole over a million dollars. Well, we will have to wait for Tony to give us a report.

SCENE 15

Peter goes to the parish rectory in pouring rain and rings the doorbell. Door opens.

FATHER VALENTINE O'BRIAN
What a surprise, Peter Metcalf, come in, come in.

PETER
Hello Father O'Brian.

O'BRIAN
What brings you out on a day like this?

PETER
My conscience, maybe?

O'BRIAN
Well you come to the right place Peter. We do make repairs on peoples consciences. Last time we talked you were filed with agnostic beliefs and I felt the church was loosing you. I prayed for you to come back to the church and here you are.

PETER
I came back thinking you might help me find answers to what is going on in my life. You heard of the accident I was in, and my paralysis.

O'BRIAN
Most people heard of your accident and I organized some prayer circles to pray for your recovery.

PETER
I heard of you organizing prayer groups for me and that is why I decided to see you about my problem.

O'BRIAN
Seems the prayers worked. You seem healthy.

PETER
Body yes, mind in doubt.

O'Brian

Would you like to go to confession about your troubles?

Peter

I am not that close to the church yet . . . I would like to just ask you some questions, and tell you what troubles me.

O'Brian

Ok.

Father O'Brian leads Peter into a conference room. And they sit down around a large table.

Peter

I have a problem understanding moral and ethical issues. Simply put, is it a sin or not? Does fair play trump morality? Is morality only applicable to individuals but not to corporations who stack all the cards in their favor?

O'Brian

Philosophers have been asking those questions for several thousand years. I can tell you that the Catholic Church follows the teachings of Christ and has a moral standard that the members of the church try to live by. Morality in different cultures, in different times varies. The Aztecs thought it was the will of God to rip out beating hearts. The Taliban believe in stoning their women for being raped.

Peter

So what you are saying, is, that anything can be moral in certain cases if society approves of it.

O'Brian

In a way, yes. You can not argue that there are different moral standards in different cultures.

Peter

If I am an agnostic then I could have my own code? No religion, no code.

O'Brian

Well, not right, in the simple fact that you are in our culture and then should make moral decisions as part of that culture.

Peter

So cultural moral standards prevail where church morality does not cover?

O'Brian

Society has rules and laws ascribing to certain moral, ethical behavior.

PETER

My question is that if insurance companies, credit card companies, banks, create rules to rip off people, cheat them, exploit them, then they set the moral standard that can be used to fight back. The people can then fight back on the moral ground established by the corporations.

O'BRIAN

You sure forgot what Jesus said about turning the other cheek. What about forgiving your enemies?

PETER

That is true for the Catholic but has nothing to do with the agnostic. No one told me to turn the other cheek or forgive. I want to use the same rules against the corporations that they use against all the little people.

O'BRIAN

Peter you surely did not need a confession nor did you need, a priest.

PETER

I needed someone from my life to tell me right from wrong. I do things that I consider morally right, just in the present time, that I would have believed to be wrong in my Catholic past life.

O'BRIAN

Peter you know what Jesus teaches. You went to all the Catholic schools and you know what you have been thought. If you do not believe that Jesus is the son of God you still know his teachings on morality are good for all the people.

PETER

All I know is that Jesus threw out all the business men from the temple, the money changers. If he was here today he would do the same with all of the rip off artists running the corporate money mills.

O'BRIAN

I do not know how to help you Peter. I am glad you came and we talked, that could be the light at the end of the dark tunnel of your life.

PETER

At this moment I do not know if the light is an end to darkness or a train coming at me. Thank you Father, and I hope to see you again when I am more settled in my mind.

O'BRIAN

I will pray for you and hope to see you soon.

They walk out the door and the rain has stopped and they look at a rainbow.

SCENE 16

This is in the Chicago office of the FBI. A conference room filled with the following people: FBI supervisor Virgil Ghlitly, Romanova Smith, his personal secretary taking notes, FBI agent Zita Washington, FBI agent Saul Levinson, General Gint Soltis, Major Al Glavin, Colonel Keith Larmon and Professor Joe Abbot and Ms Rita Lenska.

VIRGIL

You all introduced yourselves before we got into the conference room so let me start this meeting by telling you that this meeting was requested by the general here. What originally started here in Chicago, and also in Washington DC as a series of bizarre crimes, and events that seemed of no great consequence have now morphed into a possible homeland security situation.

GENERAL

Thank you all for coming and I have to tell you that this phenomenon or crime blitz is developing fast, it is also imperative that this is kept as top secret. The rumors about this must not get into the conspiracy, nut case, hands. Virgil can you please bring us right up to date on this.

VIRGIL

Well the Chicago police seemed to have a person of interest, a Doctor Fisbein, a psychiatrist, who seems to know something about the Chicago area weird crimes. The doctor was questioned by army intelligence but refused to divulge any facts except for the fact that he is possibly treating someone who is involved. The army intelligence has asked the doctor to meet with them and bring a lawyer.

GENERAL

The good doctor does not realize the powers of the Patriot Act. WE do not need any search warrants, any judges signing some scraps of paper. The doctor should be made aware that when homeland security is in any way threatened, all rules are off the table and the doctor will find himself in Poland, Bulgaria or Lithuania spilling his guts out to interrogators there who have no qualms or rules on torture. Let me just say that the criminals in Chicago and Washington who have been stealing and disappearing can also possibly enter top secret government agencies and steal there. This could be a huge disaster

VIRGIL

Romanova please leave your notes here and go back to your office. I will record this meeting on camera, thank you.

The secretary seems a little confused and leaves

GENERAL

Coming to the point here, I would like to ask our two experts on the paranormal if they have anything new to add.

ABBOT

Rita and I have researched various legends and events and find that the so called weird crimes or events have been with us through our known history. If you read the transcripts of our last meeting you will get most of the ideas on this shape shifting, and out of body travel phenomenon. One of the first times shape shifting in man or Gods is mentioned is in Greek mythology. It is the Callisto Affect, in Greek mythology, an Arcadian nymph was transformed into a bear and saved by Zeus from hunters in the forest, and carried up to the skies where she was placed as the bear constellation. So my point is that shape shifting, and out of body travel have been with us forever. Stories, myths, legends, rumors, all have some seeds of truth. They can not appear from nothing.

GENERAL

So when we have no real answers we fall back on what?

ABBOT

We fall back on answers we do not like. Answers, that question our reality. Rita and I have dug trough a lot of old records and have always arrived at the same spot. When there is something that is happening that can not be explained in the scientific approach, then we have to cross over into the realm of imagination. We have to say something is happening, we can not explain it, and that is all.

RITA

The professor is right on how to look at this. We have to simply say, it is happening, it has happened before. I am sure that we will find out how and why in the near future. The fact that apparitions appear in Chicago and Washington and that a Doctor Fishbein seems to know something here, and two vets in Washington seem as good suspects, I would say we have to step back and let the investigators nail down some real facts from the doctor and the vets.

ABBOT

I think our postulations on the ability of these people to manipulate the basic building blocks of everything that exists must be proven to us by the perpetrators themselves. Their ability it seems is to shape the so called Leibnitz Monad or God particle at will and do out of body travel. We can not get any proof without their help.

RITA

The only advice I have to offer that might be of help is that the out of body travelers have to leave their body someplace so they can return to it at will. I personally believe that their travel out of body is limited by a time factor. Their so called spirit must return to the body for restructuring.

Their body when left will be like the bodies of saints that never decompose. The spirits of these saints dissolved into the particle universe and left the body in a waiting mode.

GENERAL

Wow, that is some theory Ms. Lenska., thank you.

VIRGIL

What do you suggest we do if we locate the Chicago character and what about the vets in Washington?

RITA

I suggest that when you have these people in your hands, you sedate them into a deep sleep and try to figure out how to control them. The best solution would be to get them to cooperate with us.

GENERAL

I already issued orders to pick up this doctor.

VIRGIL

In order to confuse the curious media hounds and put them off the real story, I have put in plan B, B is for bullshit. I have instructed my operatives to leave traces of money, computer chips, mini camera parts, projector pieces, transmitter pieces to be found by my agents and to give to the Chicago police, to create an image of a realistic crime spree, using high tech instruments.

GENERAL

This will get rid of the weird crime seekers and conspiracy nuts. This will give us time to get the real story. Thank you all for your efforts, and please let us all pretend it is just a normal crime spree.

Scene fades out as people stand up and get ready to leave.

SCENE 17

Dr Fishbein is walking down Michigan Ave. when a large dark car pulls up next to the sidewalk and two plain clothes army intelligence men get out from the car and stop Doctor Fishbein.

FIRST MAN

Dr. Fishbein?

DR. FISHBEIN

Yes

SECOND MAN

Could you do us a big favor and come with us. We have a few questions we need answers for.

Fishbein does not want to get into car and says

DR. FISHBEIN

Who are you guys?

FIRST MAN

Army Intelligence Doctor. Our people talked to you before.

They show their ID's

DR. FISHBEIN

I know army intelligence I met them before, and we agreed to meet with my lawyer to answer some questions.

FIRST MAN

Sorry about the rush but we have some people from Washington who are here today and would like to meet you. This is an emergency.

DR. FISHBEIN

Let me contact my lawyer and I will meet you today.

SECOND MAN

No can do. We have orders to bring you in right now, and you can call the lawyer from the offices to meet you there. Please get into the car.

Dr. Fishbein

I will not. You have no right to force me to go with you.

First Man

It is not going to look real good if we drag you into the car, so please get in.

Fishbein reluctantly gets into the auto and says:

Dr. Fishbein

Can I use my phone to call my Lawyer?

First Man

You are going to FBI headquarters to meet General Soltis and you can make your calls then.

SCENE 18

Takes place in the Chicago Offices of the FBI. The head of the Chicago office, Virgil Ghlitly, and General Soltis are sitting Facing Dr. Fishbein.

VIRGIL

Doctor this is General Gint Soltis. He had to see you right away, so thank you for coming.

DR. FISHBEIN

I was forced to come and I will complain to the authorities.

SOLTIS

Well we are here so you go ahead and complain, please.

VIRGIL

Please, let us not start on the wrong foot.

DR. FISHBEIN

WE already are on the wrong foot.

SOLTIS

All we want to know is who are you treating related to the weird crimes in this area?

DR. FISHBEIN

That is a doctor patient private matter. I have nothing to do with weird crimes.

SOLTIS

Doctor I am involved with army intelligence and all the government agencies are wired together to protect the homeland. Nothing you can offer in disputing our rights can trump the Patriot act or homeland security. So you will answer what we ask of you or you will be on an army plane to Bulgaria or Lithuania and you will answer there. They know how to get answers.

DR. FISHBEIN

You are threatening me, an American in America. This is crazy

SOLTIS

You are right about that. It is a crazy situation, we need answers, now.

DR. FISHBEIN

I see, I have no choice here.

SOLTIS

Please Doctor, help us out with some answers, and you will never hear from us again, see us again.

DR. FISHBEIN

Can I please use the bathroom.

VIRGIL

Of course doctor.

As Doctor Fishbein gets into the bathroom, which is down the hall he takes out his phone and calls Peter Metcalf.

DR. FISHBEIN

Peter, this is Fishbein, I am with the Chicago FBI and the army Intelligence.

PETER

What do they want?

DR FISHBEIN

They want to get a hold of you. I suspect they believe you can do some of the things you claim.

Virgil enters bathroom and hears the doctor.

DR. FISHBEIN

They will figure out who you are, pack and go hide.

Virgil kicks in door of stall and tries to grab phone. Doctor drops phone in toilet and flushes.

VIRGIL

You son of a bitch. We tried dealing with you in a polite way and you go fucking us up.

DR. FISHBEIN

You break my constitutional rights, and then talk to me about politeness.

VIRGIL

Write a complaint to Senator Ron Paul, he will help you.

Fishbein is brought back to the meeting room.

SOLTIS

What happened?

VIRGIL

He fucking made a phone call in the bathroom and then flushed the phone.

SOLTIS

Nice work Virgil.

VIRGIL

I already signaled my two agents to get into his offices and grab all his patient files.

DR FISHBEIN

You can not do that.

VIRGIL

We are doing it and you are going into a safe house where you can watch Dancing With The Stars until you grow old or decide to play nice with us.

Dr. fishbein is escorted out and Virgil tells Soltis:

VIRGIL

We will have the files here within the hour and I will have five agents go through them, and we should be able to get the name he was not divulging, and pick the prick up and have him here in the afternoon.

SOLTIS

Sounds like you are on top of this. How about the false trails in all the crime locations? Is this detective Duffy getting confused enough?

VIRGIL

WE left enough shit, computer, camera, parts, in all the places and my guys, plus the local cops have been bringing all this crap to Duffy.

SOLTIS

Well I hope we can figure out this problem, and begin to control it, before the news media creates a circus for all of us.

SCENE 19

Starts in Peter Metcalf's house. Peter and Janet are packing as fast as they can. They are stuffing money and jewelry into suitcases.

PETER

Janet, hurry, please take all the money and jewelry, few clothes, we can buy all the rest.

JANET

Fast as I can. Which car are we taking?

PETER

Ferrari.

JANET

Very noticeable.

PETER

Fishbein is in trouble. I think the FBI or whatever, is racing here.

JANET

My God.

They continue packing their stuff in a red Ferrari Testarosa and start pulling out of their driveway. Two unmarked cars are coming their way on the street and attempt to block their entrance into the street. Peter backs up the Ferrari as if to stop in the driveway but suddenly turns unto the lawn and cuts across a dozen manicured front yards to gain access to the street. The pursuit starts with the two sedans chasing the Ferrari.

Heading south on Lake Shore Drive the Ferrari jumps curbs goes through parks and playgrounds with the two sedans and now joined by two police cars also in pursuit.

The pursuers now call in an overhead copter to chase them also. Peter knowing he is being followed from air also, heads downtown and turns into lower Wacker Drive to get rid of air surveillance. Meanwhile a terrible thunder storm starts out and there is a blinding rain. The copter has to leave and the Ferrari in lower Wacker Drive looses the pursuing cars. Peter ends up heading southwest on I 55 in the blinding rain storm. They exit around Joliet and as the rain stops Peter drops of Janet at a restaurant near a car dealership. He gives her four thousand dollars and tells her to buy a car for a little less than that. He also tells her he will call her cell phone and tell her directions where to pick him up.

SCENE 20

Takes place as Janet enters a car dealership. Janet is greeted by a jovial older fat man with a big belly. She glances into his office and sees that he was watching a porno movie. The guy steps back in his office and shuts TV off. Introduces himself as Chas the deal maker.

CHAS
You are a lucky lady.

JANET
How so?

CHAS
Anyone that walks into my dealership never walks out. They drive out. We do not care about your credit, your job, we are here to put you in a car.

JANET
Well sounds like I am in the right place. I have to have a car right now to go see my very sick mother in Kentucky and I can not wait for a bus tomorrow.

CHAS
We pride ourselves on pleasing the costumer.

The scene unwinds as they walk through the lot looking at different cars. At last Janet picks out a silver older Honda Accord sedan. Chas starts it for her and tells her the good points and praises the car.

JANET
Price shown is 3999, how much can you knock off if I pay cash right now?

CHAS
For a nice lady like you, in an emergency, how about 200 dollars.

JANET
Write up the papers and I will give you the money.

They enter the office and Chas starts the paperwork. As Janet sits waiting her phone rings. Peter tells her where to pick him up at his friend's farm. Janet pays Chas for the car

SCENE 21

Janet following Peter's instructions drives down country roads and turns into a farm yard. Here she sees Peter waving to her and a man dressed in bibs looking her way. She gets out of the car and approaches the two men.

PETER

How did it go?

JANET

No problems.

PETER

This is my old friend Joe. We used to do a lot of pheasant hunting on his dad's farm, now Joe does a little farming and works in town as a teacher.

JANET

Hi Joe

Joe nods a hello.

JOE

You are Janet. Nice to meet you.

PETER

Janet I told Joe about our legal and financial problems and asked Joe to help us out.

JANET

You What??

PETER

I will explain everything to you in the car. We have to get going.

JOE

Peter you are sure I will not get into any trouble over this. I will keep the Ferrari in my barn and six months later register it as my own, you signed over the title.

PETER

The Ferrari is mine and I legally sign it over to you, no problem. If I come back after all my problems are over we can work out a deal for the car in some way, if I need a place to stay or some money. Meantime for helping me out, in six months you can start using the car, you will have the use of this great car for a long time, I think.

JOE

I will keep it in the barn and not mention that I saw you. I am only doing this because you were always a good honest guy, and a very good friend back then. I know you did not steal this car

Now Peter and Janet load the suitcases into the Honda and prepare to leave.

PETER

Joe please remember that mum is the word and I know I can trust my Polish friend to keep his word.

They shake hands and Peter gets in the car. As they drive off Janet speaks up.

JANET

You just fucking gave him a three hundred thousand dollar car. Are you nuts?

PETER

How many red Ferrari cars have you seen on the road? They would pick us up in a minute. The car did not cost us anything because we bought it with appropriated dollars.

If we ever solve our problems we can always make a deal with Joe if we need money or more importantly a place to stay. Do you see a day when we can not get money to buy ten Ferrari cars??

JANET

You are so right my Robin Hood. I forgot our potential earning power for a moment.

Now the Metcalfs are driving west to Las Vegas with the Honda Accord and suitcases filled with money and jewels. They see the sights as they stop in great places, parks, casinos and fine dinning. In the hotels they rent the best rooms and Janet puts on the finest clothes they buy on the way and at night dresses as a princess with all the jewels and makes love to Peter. Peters conscience stops bothering him momentarily and Janet is like Eve in the bible leading Peter into the great life.

They eventually get to Vegas and stay at Ceasars Palace. They stay in the fanciest rooms and gamble, eat, and enjoy life. Peter tells Janet that they have to go see Doctor Mustafa in a few weeks in Mount Charleston. Which, is close to Vegas.

SCENE 22

Scene 22 takes place in the expensive suite at Ceasars.

JANET

Well my love we have finally arrived in more ways than one. Look at this place, like heaven. Heaven on earth, imagine that.

PETER

We definitely have arrived . . . now what?

JANET

Now, what? Je . . . sus . . . begin to live. All the years selling toilet paper, dealing with some lowlife to get an order, never, never having enough money to buy one per cent of what we needed, forget buying what we wanted. Look at me now, a thousand dollar dress, ten thousand in jewelry and all the workers falling all over to please us and you say, so what.

She dances around the rooms showing off her dress and jewels.

JANET

Let us go see all the shows, let us gamble, let us go eat the most expensive foods, let us shop in all the overpriced stores, begin to really live Peter.

PETER

I just feel I do not belong here.

JANET

You worked honestly and hard all your life and got nothing for it. Remember after the accident we were broke, had nothing and could not even get insurance for you. We were so screwed by life and then the miracle happened with Doctor Mustafa's drugs. Your dreams, your out of body travels made you a demi-god. I did not believe you could do this, nor did Dr. Fishbein. Who are you hurting, some race track, some insurance whores, some banks?

You have hurt no individuals only entities that hurt and exploit individuals. You are the modern day Robin Hood, and we are the poor you helped.

PETER

You make everything sound alright, but I still feel a twinge of guilt.

JANET

Jesuus, Maary, and Joseph what has to happen for you to get of this guilt trip? Ok, ok, then open up a free soup kitchen here in Vegas and help all the bums get a meal. Will that make you feel less guilty?

PETER

Will you help make the soup?

JANET

You know, you are nuts.

PETER

Nuts or not I do love you and allow you to lead me into a life of sin. Just like Eve did to Adam in the Bible story.

JANET

You do not know your Bible. Eve got Adam fucked up, and both got thrown out of paradise. I, my dear, have led you out of poverty, misery, into paradise.

PETER

You are right in a way, we are in a paradise. All that is left for me to do is to get you to introduce me to God.

JANET

I will work on locating God and in the meantime maybe Doctor Mustafa can enhance my brain to be like you. I want to travel out of body and take what I want.

PETER

According to Doctor Mustafa, when I talked to him, you have to be clinically dead for a little while, and then take the stem cell derivatives to affect and change your brain.

JANET

I would be willing to try it.

PETER

I can already get all you want. What else would you need?

JANET

You just do not get it. You have no imagination Peter. You have power greater than a nuclear bomb.

PETER

Maybe no one should have such power until the human race grows up, matures, to be able to control such power.

JANET

You control it?

PETER

Is that what you call it? Robbing, and stealing is under control?

JANET

Yes, you are controlling it.

PETER

Would you control it? Would the dark side of Janet take over and try to shape the world according to Janet? I know your politics and your feelings about what is wrong with the world. I believe you would embark on a crusade to remake the world to your image or what you think it should be.

JANET

Maybe I would try to correct some wrongs, so what?

PETER

You see how horrible it would be to take away rights from an elected government and to manipulate things to your desires. You would be an invisible dictator.

JANET

To right some wrongs would be wrong according to you?

PETER

Might does not make right.

JANET

Let us go have fun, I do not want to argue or debate with you.

The room scene ends as they leave to go have fun.

SCENE 23

Takes place in Chicago police precinct where detective Duffy is meeting with His associates Maurice Ward and Ann Bic.

DUFFY

Well like they say closure is always good on what ails you. Per orders,we are disbanding this unit and closing the investigation on the weird crime spree.

ANN

I do not believe what I am hearing.

DUFFY

Not my decision, it comes from the very top. The top got the word from higher up, if you can believe.

MAURICE

This is pure bullshit. We were just lining up all of our ducks in a row to get answers.

ANN

Maurice is right. The crimes have not been solved.

DUFFY

They will not be solved to our satisfaction, I think. FBI has given our labs some realy high tech fragments from the crime scenes that we supposedly missed finding. These so called pieces of evidence imply a high tech scam perpetrated by some evil computer, or surveillance experts.

ANN

Duffy, you know this is all bullshit. We swept those places clean. There was nothing.

DUFFY

That is not what the FBI state in their reports. The army intelligence is satisfied with the FBI reports, and they ask for this investigation to be closed. They also want the fragment evidence and all of our files, to study in depth, this high tech crime.

MAURICE

We did not get a chance to talk to Dr. Fishbein.

DUFFY

Dr. Fishbein has been missing for a whole week.

MAURICE

This case should not be closed.

DUFFY

Ok, Maurice why don't you talk to the police chief and the FBI. As far as head of this team I am telling you it is closed.

ANN

This is all wrong Duffy, and you know it.

DUFFY

Whatever, you are both off this ended project and will receive new assignments in a few days.

MAURICE

This is bullshit and the sad fact is that we all know it is bullshit.

SCENE 24

Virgil Ghlitly and General Soltis in Chicago FBI office.

SOLTIS

I understand you left the evidence in the crime scenes to confuse everybody.

VIRGIL

Just like homeland security and army intelligence asked. I do want to express a protest of my own as to the way this is handled. We can not become a nation of liars, and cheats. A nation where people like Dr. Fishbein disappears and you do not have an idea when you might release him. I promised to put him in a safe house but you got him moved to God knows where.

SOLTIS

Dr. fishbein will be released from our custody when the information he has becomes of no interest to anybody and he comes to an understanding of what potential dangers we face.

VIRGIL

We, you, as our government, leave false evidence, kidnap people, lie to the press and still seem to think we are a free and moral nation.

SOLTIS

No one likes doing this shit but we have no other option. If this patient of Doctor Fishbein can do this out of body travel shit and Russia or China got a hold of him, how long do you think this nation would be free? Things have changed and so must we. We are fighting terrorists with possible weapons of mass destruction. Would you still question our right to torture an individual if one of our cities faced a nuclear threat from what the terrorist knows?

VIRGIL

So our laws, morals, ethics go out the window if we perceive a threat, or you perceive a threat?

SOLTIS

You got the picture. Under the Patriot Act, and the Homeland Security all morals are off the table and our survival trumps everything.

VIRGIL

So what do we do now?

SOLTIS

You turn your files over to my people, you tell the agents working on this, that the police have evidence working with army intelligence that it was a techno type scam. You transfer your agents to other areas, split them up and end the investigation.

VIRGIL

But they will know we planted the stuff.

SOLTIS

That is where your great leadership qualities will show and you will also leak information to the papers of a techno scam being solved. I in turn will recommend you for bigger jobs in Washington.

VIRGIL

Will I also get thirty pieces of silver?

SOLTIS

You know there was a more sure way of ending these investigations. People get heart attacks, have accidents. Let us close this weird shit on a happy note, a little lie.

VIRGIL

Having your health, I guess trumps a lot of things. What happens to the two vets in Washington?

SOLTIS

They are alive and well under close supervision. They will not be doing a lot of out of body traveling. We also have a Doctor Mustafa under surveillance and believe he is the one who treated Dr. Fishbein's patient. We worked well together and I have a lot of respect for you and your people and would like to close this out on a win, win, ending. I also would like you to do me a favor and talk to professor Abbot and this Vampirella. Please tell them it was all a techno type crime. Then please forget the whole thing ever happened.

VIRGIL

General I will do what you ask, but you and I will never sleep soundly because we know what happened and can happen again.

SCENE 25

This scene takes place in Walter Reed Hospital. The administrator of the hospital is present, Vito Simtestis, and a lady doctor Donna Artz, along with General Soltis, Major Al Glavin and Colonel Keith Larmon.

SOLTIS

Thank you Vito for taking the time out to meet with us.

VITO

Glad to be of help.

SOLTIS

To bring you up to date on our two vets in question, Sergio Sanches and David Repsy I have to report to all of you that since I asked Doctor Artz to sedate the two vets, and keep them sedated, we have had no mysterious events in or around the hospital. Strange is it not? Dr. Artz maybe you could give us more information on the two vets in question?

ARTZ

More than happy to do so general. It seems that the two vets were brought to us from Iraq where they were almost killed with a roadside bomb. First army aid wrote them off as dead but then because of our fantastic medications and modern techniques they were both resuscitated. This is the case in Iraq, our wounded survive as a larger percent when compared to other wars. That is why on roughly four thousand dead we have over forty thousand maimed survivors.

SOLTIS

So they were brought here and put in your care.

ARTZ

They were paralyzed from the neck down. We did a lot of cosmetic surgery to make them look human and we measured all their functions and recorded them. A doctor Mustafa was on our staff working to rehabilitate the paralyzed vets and try to restore some functions to them.

SOLTIS

Can we meet this doctor Mustafa?

VITO

He disappeared after we discovered he was experimenting and using embryonic stem cell drug concoctions not approved in the US.

ARTZ

It seemed, he was without consulting the hospital, pumping stem cell cocktails into these two vets. Using them to experiment.

SOLTIS

So no one knew that this was going on.

ARTZ

Correct, until we saw an improvement in the two vets. They started moving around, this was an impossible event according to us. We gave them brain scans and it showed a huge amount of abnormal activity. Their brains seemed super activated, super alert. We asked doctor Mustafa what drugs he gave the two vets. The only thing he told us was that he was trying to help them get well by giving them some illegal stem cell extractions from southeast Asia. He told us that the drugs were not yet approved here but he would give us the complete file the next day. He also asked us if we were not happy that the two vets seemed to be recovering from a diagnosed paralysis.

SOLTIS

So this doctor never showed up the next day and never gave you any files, and all you had were two recovering vets that you had written off as impossible cases for recovery from paralysis?

VITO

After doctor Mustafa disappeared with his file, strange things started happening. Things started disappearing from the hospital and in the areas around the hospital. We placed guards in the corridors, no one came or left, yet stolen objects were found and recovered in Sergio's and David's room.

ARTZ

There is no way stolen stuff could have come into their room. Yet surveillance cameras had tapes of the vets, and their fingerprints were found at the crime scenes, the tapes showed the two vets walking, laughing and stealing, yet the guards in the corridors swear no one left their room.

SOLTIS

Thank you for your input. The army intelligence unit will take the sedated vets into their care, and move them to a special location with more supervision. The weird crime thieving episodes have also occurred in Chicago as you all know, and have been explained as a high tech crime scam perpetrated by some computer geeks, evidence was found at the scenes indicating that.

ARTZ

What about the out of body travel theory thrown around?

SOLTIS

It was thrown out.

ARTZ

I can not release these men to you from my care because we have a moral, ethical, reason to keep them here and figure out what drug cured these men from permanent paralysis. We could help many paralyzed people if we figure out how these men recovered.

SOLTIS

Dear doctor, I understand your position and desire to help other paralyzed people but an illegal procedure was used as an experiment on our beloved vets. They were under your supervision and were used as experimental lab animals by some weirdo doctor who now disappeared. I could look at this as an act of terrorism was committed on your watch.

ARTZ

They were cured, saved from a life of being vegetables, and we can cure others if we figure out what doctor Mustafa gave them. You can not take away a cure, stop research, just because you have the might on your side. Why can you not simply leave us alone to continue this research and do what you do best, continue your wars. Must you now involve yourself with stopping cures and research. When will your uniformed types, and the religious fanatics get off the backs of the human race and let research help end suffering. I will go to the news media and expose your actions in preventing possible cures for paralysis

VITO

Doctor, please.

SOLTIS

Dear Doctor Artz if you do this, we will have you arrested as a terrorist for doing experiments on healthy vets who were misdiagnosed by you, purposely. We will get Muslim inmates to swear you were paid money, to screw this country and torture our vets. We will deposit money in your name in different accounts. We can do all of that. This fucking meeting is over. Also doctor you can write to me from Bulgaria if they give you a pencil and a stamp to mail a letter and tell me how much you hate our procedures to protect the homeland.

VITO

Jesus, sorry, everybody, all that's left to say is, how about them Steelers.

SCENE 26

The Metcalfs are having a great time in Vegas. They have contacted Dr. Mustafa and he has come to Caesars to meet with them in their suite. The doctor is impressed with the surroundings.

DOCTOR

Well Peter you and Janet have come a long way . . . economically that is.

JANET

All of it thanks to you.

DOCTOR

I only cured the paralysis, that is all.

PETER

Funny you never mentioned the side effects of your stem cell cocktails you gave me.

JANET

Usually the medicine has warnings, like, will cause impotence or a rash.

PETER

You left it up to us to discover the side effects of your drug. I almost went insane trying to figure out what is happening to me when I fall asleep.

JANET

I believed he did go insane until he started to show up with expensive items and cash.

DOCTOR

So I cured your paralysis and made you into an unstoppable super thief.

JANET

Peter is like my private Robin Hood. He only steals from corporations and insurance companies. They rip us off and we take some back.

DOCTOR

Stealing is stealing no matter how you try to put a spin on it.

PETER

My conscience has been bothering me and I have considered asking you if you can stop this ability of out of body travel.

JANET

No fucking way Peter. What is wrong with you? I wanted to ask the doctor to make me like you. Give me the ability.

DOCTOR

Let me explain what we are playing with. The stem cell derivatives that were banned in your country by a religious misguided president were legal in the more enlightened countries. I believed it was immoral to have some religious freaks with their religious false illusions stop possible cures for sick people. I sacrificed my career, my practice, my reputation and became a fugitive because I was intent on curing people.

PETER

When did you figure out the out of body travel phenomena?

DOCTOR

I figured out this when I started giving my cure to the two vets at Walter Reed. I looked over their file and saw that they were clinically dead in Iraq. They were hit in their vehicle by a bomb and were for all purposes dead. Their life signs were gone but because of the fast emergency response, they were resuscitated. In your case it was the same thing. I have used my drugs on several paralyzed people and cured them with no side effects. These people with no side effects were never clinically dead, they were only paralyzed.

JANET

So you have to die momentarily to somehow lay the ground for your stem cell medicine to get the effect of out of body travel.

DOCTOR

That seems the step necessary to have this side effect. I personally believe that the mind is purged at the moment of death of all the useless clutter we have and it somehow becomes pure energy and unites with the basic building blocks of the universe. Science today points us in the direction that the universe is made up of tiny particles. The so called God Particle. This is the smallest building block of all that exists. These particles are discovered by smashing the known small particles and what splinters, is theorized as this basic building block.

PETER

What has this God Particle to do with me?

DOCTOR

When people experience this flat line type death they all claim they saw a light of some kind. They claim they felt comfortable and happy in going toward this light. This is only my theory but I believe that our soul or very essence is a compacted sphere of energy, God Particles that are contained in our mind. We grow and accumulate this essence in our lifetime and when we die we release this very essence of ourselves, our soul so to speak, into the total sea of energy around us.

PETER

So what happened to me?

DOCTOR

You were through the gate into the sea of energy and because you were not allowed to stay dead you came back. You had a glimpse of how the total essence of the universe works. You were like a spy that comes back home with information. You saw momentarily the universe of many shapes and forms all created by the ever shifting God Particles. You mastered their ability to manipulate your own energy particles. First subconsciously then willfully you were able to leave certain particles and flow with others to your destinations.

PETER

I do not think you know how to stop this . . . do you?

DOCTOR

I do not.

JANET

Sounds like I do not want to try this.

DOCTOR

I have not tried it on myself. I do not think I will ever do it, maybe.

PETER

Where does that leave the belief in the traditional concept of God?

DOCTOR

I can only tell you what my personal belief is. God is the total of all the energy or God Particles in everything that exists, and his way of thinking is the process of shaping everything that exists in the universe. He is the sum total of all God Particles and he shapes all existing forms into what they are. All things change, planets, furniture, living things, all, revert at some time to basic energy particles. The only thing we know is that possibly, energy can not be created nor destroyed. So the sum total of God Particles remains the same. The shaping of all the forms, and what they do, is what we might call intelligent design, or God's way of thinking.

PETER

What about morality?

DOCTOR

Morality is in the eye of the beholder. I personally do believe there can be acts that are evil. I also believe that ancient religions and the dying modern day religious illusions peck away at the concept of good and evil. Religion also tries to present a fantasy of punishment or reward after life to substantiate morality. I can also include that in my concept of a God Particle universe the dying person, as we said, now gives up his essence, soul, of contained God Particles. His basic entity, again soul, our concept of the I, is now poured into the universe of all God Particles. How is our personal quantity of energy, our soul, our God Particles, received by the whole. If we live an evil life and die, it is like putting something smelly, dirty into the whole pot of energy. Maybe that can be an understanding of hell or heaven?

PETER

I am not unconfused.

JANET

Can I get more drinks?

DOCTOR

The reason I believe we are confused is that our thinking process is completely different from the God Particle universe. The God Particles create and shape forms, but we can only perceive their shapes and attributes.

We can look at an ant hill and ask ourselves weather the ants can understand us. We must also ask ourselves if we care if some ants steal from other ants. We must look at the distance between us and ants and then we look at the distance between us and the concept of God in the particle theory and we can see our limitations in comprehending God. We are much closer in physique, instinct, needs, activities to the ant and yet we care nothing about how the ants treat each other or commit crimes against each other.

God certainly does not think like we do, he simply is ever forming and creating all that exists. Our ability to reason, and now your ability to manipulate some of these building blocks is a step closer to merging and discovering a lonely God. The Gnostics of two thousand years ago believed that our minds were the parts of God we were meant to develop to achieve an understanding of God. They believed in the ability to reason versus an organized religion telling us what God wants and is.

PETER

So where does that leave me?

DOCTOR

Well your abilities are very dangerous. You can see what foreign powers would do to get you in their hands. You can imagine how our own country would try to use you in international affairs. You are the perfect spy, the perfect assassin. Your life would not be your own. I would recommend that you go into very deep hiding.

PETER

Spend my life with Janet as some sort of mutant fugitives.

DOCTOR

That is one way of looking at the problem. Weigh your options. You could go work for the government.

PETER

I can not keep gambling and having this crazy life here in Vegas.

JANET

I like this life.

PETER

You will get bored at some time.

DOCTOR

Peter is right Janet.

JANET

So what do you recommend good doctor?

DOCTOR

Peter has a great gift. Use it to do good, help mankind. You can figure out how to do this, it will give you a purpose and a reason to live. Do the opposite of what Paris Hilton does.

PETER

What are you doing?

DOCTOR

I am working on one of my countrymen to send him into an area of the world that needs some good works.

PETER

Sounds that you have a personal agenda for this power.

DOCTOR

Not for my benefit, you know me. I have a lab near by in another town, Mount Charleston. I will call you in a couple of weeks. If you go into hiding do not let me know where. I am still not sure if the authorities are looking for me.

Doctor leaves

JANET

This is all so weird, let us go and live.

SCENE 27

Takes place in the Metcalf's suite. Janet is sitting on the sofa holding her head and Peter is walking back and forth.

PETER

I asked you not to drink so much. Look at you, completely wasted in the middle of the day.

JANET

I am fine, just a headache.

PETER

We got to talk about what the hell we are doing here.

JANET

We are having fun, fun, fun.

PETER

I am getting bored and so are you, and you know it.

JANET

I am not bored.

PETER

You are drunk or buzzed all the time, and I know you have been using coke.

JANET

You do not love me anymore.

PETER

I love you very much, that is why we have to talk and change.

JANET

I like this life.

PETER

This is not life. We exist here progressing into what?

JANET

Is having fun so wrong? Is unlimited pleasure so wrong?

PETER

How can I make you see that we are becoming jaded and we need to increase our pleasure degree to a higher level constantly. You are into booze and drugs. I have gambled and gambled and find it meaningless. Money is not money to me because we have an unlimited supply of it. It is meaningless pieces of paper. What do I care if I win a hundred thousand or loose that much? I can go places and pick up all the money I want.

JANET

Then obviously if you are bored with it all, do something different. Open a fucking soup kitchen and feed all the bums.

PETER

I considered doing different things but I want us to be together.

JANET

Go cook your soup just come home at night and hold me. I need that very much.

PETER

I wanted to talk to you about a letter I received from doctor Mustafa.

JANET

Does he say anything about giving me the ability you have?

PETER

No, he does not mention you. He has been running experiments on my situation and has I believe created one other person, besides the two veterans in Walter Reed hospital, that can do what I can do. You know he is of Lebanese parents and has a soft spot for the people suffering in Lebanon, and the Middle East. He claims he has created a holy warrior and sent him there to right what he sees as unfairness. He sounds in his letter that the person he transformed has no idea how he was transformed but sees himself as a holy warrior with a mission.

JANET

This person in the Middle East could cause unbelievable harm to any balance that exists there.

PETER

This power is obviously affecting Mustafa and in the letter he seems to believe he is the Mahdi with a mission to fix or save the world.

JANET

What the hell is a Mahdi?

PETER

It is a temporal or spiritual leader in that area. I believe Mustafa will get enough courage to get my type of ability for himself. I think he is confused and becoming dangerous. He believes that this is a step in mankind's evolution that will be like the second coming in the Bible.

JANET

I can see how you think this can be a problem. A thousand people like you could turn the world we know upside-down.

PETER

He also tells me not to stay out of body longer than one hour. He believes that the actual form of the human body that gives shape to our out of body form is connected. The out of body form will begin to lose the form we have shaped by our real body when we are away from it too long. The out of body form will begin to dissolve, and merge into what he believes is the total sum of all that exists in the universe. Simply put our collection of God Particles in the shape of our body begins to loose this form if we are away from the sleeping body for a longer time. Our out of body form, or essence ceases to exist as a separate entity in the universe of God Particles. We merge with them. This he claims is what happens when we die, we simply merge into the total of all that exists. You can think of it as a drop of rain that has a shape, a form, and then falls into a pond of water. The drop shape, form, is gone but the quantity of water from the drop now became a part of the water in the pond.

JANET

Sounds like he wants to argue with all the concepts of existing religions and start his own.

PETER

I believe if he is allowed to produce people with my powers he can accomplish anything.

JANET

What happens to the body if the so called entity does not return?

PETER

Mustafa seemingly tracked down a professor Abbot that was mentioned in our weird crime escapades in Chicago and got some weird answers.

JANET

Who is this Abbot?

PETER

Abbot is a paranormal researcher. That told Mustafa that this out of body phenomenon is as old as man's history. He mentioned to Mustafa shape shifters and saints whose bodies never decompose. Mustafa seems to believe that if the traveler out of body disappears, the body never decomposes as it waits for the return. Also there is the myth that vampires who shift shapes have to come back every night to their coffins filled with their homeland dirt before daylight.

JANET

Maybe we should give all this information to the authorities?

PETER

I have to figure out what I want to do with the rest of my life. I have to see my options. I also have to tell you I invited Father Valentine to come to Vegas and talk to me. I sent him a plane ticket.

JANET

You never even bothered asking me how I would feel about this priest coming here. What if he contacts the FBI?

PETER

He is a priest but I believe he is my friend also.

JANET

We will see, we will see. I hope he can straighten your mind out. Dr. Fishbein could not. Let us go have some great food and go sit by the pool.

SCENE 28

Father Valentine is coming to see Peter Metcalf. The scenes tied in with the 28 scene that takes place in a Caesars restaurant are a picturesque view of Vegas from the plane and then Father Valentine's scenic drive on the strip with a limo that Peter sent to pick him up at the airport. Father is amazed at the Luxury of Caesars hotel and decides to remove his collar as not to attract attention. He goes to a men's room and as he starts to remove the collar a black attendant says to him.

BLACK ATTENDANT

Welcome to Caesars Father. We have different colognes can I show you some?

VALENTINE

Thank you I do not use cologne.

BLACK ATTENDANT

I do not see too many priests in Vegas.

VALENTINE

Maybe they remove their collars?

BLACK ATTENDANT

I guess gambling and having a good time is not a good example for your flock, so you remove your collar.

VALENTINE

You are a nosy guy, but I can see how your job can become rather boring. People come and go having fun and here you are.

BLACK ATTENDANT

I only stay here about six hours get paid well, get good tips, and enjoy talking to a great mix of people. I hope you do not mind me being nosy, but I have never seen a priest in here removing his collar.

VALENTINE

It just seemed to me a collar would attract attention and maybe upset some people.

BLACK Attendant

We get all kind of people here, some in their ethnic dress, seems no one is bothered.

VALENTINE

I just do not want to attract attention.

BLACK ATTENDANT

Well go have great time and win some money for you church.

VALENTINE

I am not here to gamble.

The attendant brushes his sports coat off and stands waiting for a tip. Valentine tips him and walks out and begins to wander around Caesars taking in the scenery. He finally enters a restaurant-bar type eatery and sits at the bar. Orders a drink and takes out his cell phone, calls Peter and tells him he is in this restaurant. As he sits waiting at the bar a beautiful woman enters the place and looks around. A moment passes and Valentine looks at her by the doorway thinking perhaps Peter and Janet have arrived. His look and smile seem to invite the woman to sit next to Valentine. She comes and sits down next to Valentine. She begins by stating her name. Marrisa.

MARRISA

Marrisa

VALENTINE

What?

MARRISA

Not what . . . that is my name.

VALENTINE

Oh, sorry. I am Father Valentine O'Brian, lot of people call me Val.

MARRISA

A real priest, you are kidding?

VALENTINE

No, I am here to see a friend about a problem he has.

MARRISA

This place is full of problem people. You should talk to the management about having a chapel at Caesars. Like you know, a Doc in the box, this would be a priest in the box for emergency situations.

VALENTINE

Now, who is kidding?

MARRISA

I guess Marrisa.

VALENTINE

You are on vacation?

MARRISA

No, I work here.

VALENTINE

What is your position?

MARRISA

My favorite is missionary.

VALENTINE

Noo . . . I mean, like what do you do here?

MARRISA

Oh, that, I am a show girl.

VALENTINE

Like an actress?

MARRISA

No, I do not have a speaking part I just strut around the stage with a lot of feathers and display my boobs.

VALENTINE

No speaking parts, just displaying your breasts and you get paid?

MARRISA

Now I know you are kidding me, you . . . know about the shows.

VALENTINE

Maybe I am just kidding you a little.

MARRISA

Here I will give you a show ticket for tonight. Come and see me perform and you can buy me a drink after the show.

VALENTINE

A tempting offer Marrisa but I have been fighting temptation, and sin, to make sure my flock and I get to heaven, the show might be a distraction.

MARRISA

We have something in common Father I have here on earth given men a taste of heaven. You know what I mean. Religion realy bothers me, I am sorry.

VALENTINE

Your name should be Eve.

MARRISA

You possibly think you are going to paradise. Your celibacy, your wet dreams, your denial of pleasures . . . is that your payment to get to paradise? The news of wars, murders, disease, starvation all around you and you think I am the evil temptress Eve, that will lead you away from your righteous path. You should be so lucky.

VALENTINE

Who are you? I mean who are you really inside your façade?

MARRISA

I will tell you. I have a PHD in Psychology but I earn a lot more money showing my boobs. I am also a fallen away Catholic so I understand your problems in having to abandon reason and trying to sort illusions, and fantasies, in your brain.

VALENTINE

I believe you need help.

MARRISA

You are cute, but I can see we are traveling in different directions. Thank you for the drink.

As Marrisa gets up and leaves, Valentine orders a double Bourbon on the rocks. He sits staring at the wall with a painting of a bunch of nymphs, partly naked, frolicking in the woods. Moments pass and then the Metcalfs walk in. They approach Valentine, greet each other and proceed to a large private luxurious booth.

SCENE 29

The restaurant in Caesars. A booth with Peter, Janet, and Valentine, sitting having drinks.

PETER

Thank you for taking the time to come see us.

VALENTINE

I am your priest and your life long friend. You also sent me a free ticket and who can pass up an opportunity for a free vacation. I also got a free ticket to this review show from this lady I met at the bar.

JANET

It is just a titty show father.

PETER

Janet, I think father knows that.

VALENTINE

Please, rest assured I am not going.

PETER

Since we last talked and I was very confused I met and talked to Doctor Mustafa trying to get some answers. I did get answers about my condition and at the same time I learned what my options are.

VALENTINE

I guess seeing how you live and have been living here in the lap of luxury I can surmise that the money keeps on rolling in.

PETER

I have stopped my showmanship money appropriations. No more masked characters appearing and confusing the cops. I simply get in, get out, and no one knows what happened.

VALENTINE

You know, it is wrong what you are doing.

PETER

Right or wrong is not what I want to talk to you about.

VALENTINE

What can be more important than the morality of an act?

PETER

It is the power of being able to do the out of body travel that scares me. The explanation that Doctor Mustafa gave me of the God Particles being manipulated at my desire. He claims it is the next step in mankind's evolution. He believes a new religion is developing, it will be a new religion based on known scientific facts and he sees the God Particles as an explanation of all that is shaped by them in the universe. He sees the building blocks as he calls them to be the very essence of God. He sees God as the total mass of energy, God Particles, constantly shaping different forms of all that exists. He sees himself in the Islamic eschtology as a Mahdi type prophet bringing about the new religion and a new evolved man. The doctor is beginning to scare me also.

VALENTINE

That is the craziest theory about God and the universe I have heard.

PETER

Crazy or not, it tries to explain what is happening to me. Our old religions with God pictured as an old man with a white beard having a son that has to be tortured and murdered and some ghost being a part of them, and all are invisible to mankind, perhaps, makes more sense to you?

VALENTINE

Peter I came here to help you not to debate.

PETER

You are right.

JANET

I think you need a referee . . . me.

VALENTINE

Maybe you are right.

JANET

Father the problem in a nut shell is that Peter is sick of living the great life here. We have everything that the richest people on this planet have. We can keep having this till the day we die and he does not want it. He is bored.

VALENTINE

Maybe the fact that he did not honestly earn it is bothering him?

PETER

That is not it Father. I have seen our politicians steal, large corporations exploit people, banks, abuse people and legally steal from them, so it is not the guilt of how I get the money. I simply am bored.

JANET

He got over the guilt but now he seems he does not like to do anything. I told him to open a soup kitchen

VALENTINE

That is a great idea. A justification of what you are, you become a Robin Hood.

PETER

You are joking? Me, open a soup kitchen, maybe.

VALENTINE

It is better than you gambling with no need to win money.

JANET

His feelings, about this great life, turns upside down my belief in the paradise that Adam and Eve lost and the heaven promised us when we die. Imagine Peter being in paradise with Adam and Eve, having everything, and then because of the original sin God says you have to leave this place, and Peter say to God, great, I was really bored here. This is what the problem is. I can also imagine us getting to heaven and Peter complaining, I am so bored here, I have everything.

VALENTINE

I can not explain your take on paradise or Heaven. I never have been in either place. I can tell you that here on earth people like to have the satisfaction of achievement. We strive to get things and when we get them we feel a sense of accomplishment. You no longer have to strive for anything. That is why you are bored.

PETER

You might be right about the wanting and striving and getting that makes people happy. I probably would have walked out of paradise without having God throw me out because I was bored there. Then there would not have been an original sin and no reason for Christ to be born, suffer and die. Imagine what that would have done to the Christian Church dogmas.

VALENTINE

I will not debate you on this subject, but I will constantly pray for you to find the road back.

PETER

I appreciate you coming here and I see your explanation on the need to want something, giving you purpose in life.

VALENTINE

Well we achieved something. The other question you had was on options for your life. I can only say to you that you should stop this life of no purpose, stop stealing, and either return the money or start doing things to help other people. This could give you a reason to live.

JANET

I do not like any of your suggestions, Father Valentine. Peter has to learn to enjoy life.

PETER

Father I am also afraid that the government will figure out that I could be used as an assassin, a weapon, a spy, and my life would not be my own. Dr. Mustafa also scares me with his experiments and the new man he envisions, and himself as the Mahdi.

VALENTINE

I have told you I will not tell anyone of our conversations. So you do not have to worry about me. I would advise you to start a normal life, have children, get a job, and do not use your shape shifting, out of body travels. You are the master of your mind and body. Ask Christ to help you as you begin to find room for him in your life.

PETER

It might be a good option.

JANET

Only, if it is a very big house with a lot of servants.

PETER

I know I do not want to get involved with government work.

VALENTINE

Then disappear, and start leading a normal life somewhere. No pun intended.

JANET

Father how long will you be staying as our guest?

VALENTINE

I will leave tomorrow mid morning.

PETER

You are sure you would not want to see more of Vegas?

VALENTINE

I came to see both of you. I have done that.

JANET

Lets us order some great food and we can maybe then go see one of those magic shows. Or maybe Peter wants to see a titty show.

PETER

I am sure Father would prefer a magic show.

VALENTINE

Magic show . . . yes.

The scene ends as they begin to order food.

SCENE 30

Mount Charleston, Nevada. High in the mountains, not far from Vegas, is a resort type community. It is full of very expensive so called second homes. Some are very large, others small, but all super expensive. Some are built into the sides of steep elevations. Small front and back yards but the views are all fantastic. The luxurious Lincoln Town car pulls up in front of one of the biggest houses and we see the driver, Colonel Keith Larmon, gets out along with Major Al Glavin. Glavin opens the door and General Gint Soltis gets out. There are several sheriff's patrol cars following and they park along side the road. The three military men, wearing side arms, proceed to the front door, while some deputies are seen walking around the back. They ring the bell and the door is opened after a little delay. We see doctor Mustafa dressed in a pure white robe.

DOCTOR MUSTAFA
Yes . . . what is it that you want?

LARMON
We want to talk with you doctor Mustafa.

DOCTOR MUSTAFA
The sheriffs police outside also want to talk to me?
(Here the Dr. points to the two officers going around the back)

SOLTIS
I am General Gint Soltis and these are my associates Major Al Glavin and Colonel Keith Larmon. We are from army intelligence and would like a word with you. Can we come in?

DOCTOR MUSTAFA
If a word is all you want, why is my home being surrounded? But, please do come in, let us not upset the neighbors.

The three military men follow the doctor into the house.

DOCTOR MUSTAFA
Let us go into the library it is more comfortable, and the mountain view is fantastic.

The library has windows with a great view, and the book shelves are filled to capacity. Soltis looks at the books and says.

SOLTIS
A lot of philosophy books.

DOCTOR MUSTAFA

Yes, I study different philosophers when I encounter difficult problems.

SOLTIS

You must have a very good idea why we are here.

DOCTOR MUSTAFA

I know why you are here, but I do not know how you found me.

SOLTIS

Easy question, our department is tied into all agencies working to protect the homeland. So we all share information and under the Patriot act we do not have to waste time to get answers. Simply put, we located Peter Metcalf's home and his telephone records and there you were talking to Peter Metcalf.

DOCTOR MUSTAFA

So you picked up Peter?

SOLTIS

We accessed your phone records from this house and located him in Vegas. He is under surveillance as we speak.

DOCTOR MUSTAFA

So what is it that you want from me?

SOLTIS

We want you to tell us about the illegal stem cell medications that you used on Metcalf and the two vets at Walter Reed. You know that they were paralyzed and you seemingly cured them.

DOCTOR MUSTAFA

I am sure you are not here about the paralysis cure.

SOLTIS

There seems to be a very weird side effect from your cure causing these three patients to be in two places at the same time. Perhaps, as explained by some experts, as an out of body travel, but with more corporeal type attributes.

DOCTOR MUSTAFA

You seem to have all the answers, I can add nothing more.

SOLTIS

You must realize that if this phenomenon of out of body traveling, brought on by your drugs is real, and other countries get this cure, and side effect, what it will do to international relations.

DOCTOR MUSTAFA

If one country has this, then we have a problem, if all countries have this, then it is a stalemate. Like the cold war, both atomic powers were afraid of each other.

SOLTIS

I do not care for your philosophical appraisals. My job is to protect the homeland at all costs. I can not under any circumstance let this situation get loose. No matter what it takes. What it costs. We must know how you did it. How many people know about this? We must have all your files.

DR.

All you have to do is ask dear General, I will tell you all I know and I am sure it will never leave this room.

SOLTIS

How?

DOCTOR MUSTAFA

It seems that my drug, a combination of stem cell variations given to paralysis patients restores severed nerves. That is all that happens to paralyzed people. However to people like Metcalf and the two vets it affected them with a very strange side affect. The reason for that side affect, I believe, is that all three were clinically dead for a minute or so.

SOLTIS

So a person clinically dead and revived and given your stem cell concoction will be able to do out of body travel? That is some warning of a side affect to put on the bottle of pills.

DOCTOR MUSTAFA

It would appear so.

SOLTIS

Do you realize what devastating results we would face if this drug of yours really does this and the information gets out even accidentally, if it is given to some one in Iran, Russia, China, North Korea that was clinically dead and paralyzed.

DOCTOR MUSTAFA

Absolutely you are right, it would end the world as we know it. So I made sure no one gets it, not even you.

SOLTIS

You are an American, Doctor, are you not?

DOCTOR MUSTAFA

I am a human being first than an American.

SOLTIS

Let me clarify for you. We aim to stop this activity of yours. We will neutralize the two vets and put them on ice so to speak. We will also get rid and isolate this creation of yours, this Frankenstein, poltergeist, Peter Metcalf who has been robbing everything imaginable.

DOCTOR MUSTAFA

So morality, our constitution, go out the window when you perceive there is a danger, real or imagined. The fact that the illegal stem cell drug can cure paralyzed people means nothing to you if there is the rare danger of the side affect occurring.

SOLTIS

We can not take chances on your side affects, so, these experiments, these cures stop right now. We have you and we want answers and your files. Also, what is this shit about the God Particle everyone is spewing about.

DOCTOR MUSTAFA

Very briefly, it is the smallest energy entity and it is the basic building block of everything that exists. Somehow by people dying, flat-lining, the brain is cleansed and then my stem cell concoction stimulates the brain to a new level of performance. The persons affected by this, develop a power to manipulate the God Particles they are made off.

SOLTIS

This is one crazy theory doctor.

DOCTOR MUSTAFA

I believe general that this is the next step in human evolution. Our race will morph into a race of energy beings. We will become a cognizant entity in the mind of God as we mingle our God Particles, yet retain our basic concept of I.

SOLTIS

I thought Abbot and Vampirella were nuts, but this takes the cake.

DOCTOR MUSTAFA

Do you believe in the Bible general?

SOLTIS

Of coarse I do.

DOCTOR MUSTAFA

I refer to the second coming. The so called Rapture. It means that mankind will be lifted up to a heavenly state when that happens.

SOLTIS

Then you doctor will have to rebuild the temple I guess. Before Christ can come down and lift us up.

DOCTOR MUSTAFA

The Bible was written by very smart people for very primitive people. Explanations had to be put in easy to understand stories. The second coming is not about the dead Christ coming, it is the whole human race transforming closer to a God like state. Free of your wars, diseases, death, this is what mankind wants. We will be free of the religions that were useful at one time but now are just so much fantasy.

SOLTIS

You really, really believe this nonsense?

DOCTOR MUSTAFA

Enough to die for it. Let me try to explain to you, because I feel we are all very much in all this together. Fellow travelers embarking on a journey of discovery. The highest form or shape that God Particles can coalesce into, is the human mind, or the concept of I. So it follows dear general that the concept of the I, the human mind, does not want to dissolve or appear as a lower form or shape after death. The I wishes to retain its highest evolutionary level, that is why the next step in human evolution is this particle shaping level.

SOLTIS

So how will you bring this next step in evolution about?

DOCTOR MUSTAFA

The world is not ready for the next step. I decided to wait for seventy five years and then release the secret to the whole world.

SOLTIS

You, you, you . . . You are nuts, who the hell do you think you are to set a time line?

DOCTOR MUSTAFA

It is my discovery, and perhaps some generations later, there will not be so many Neanderthals in charge that orchestrate stupid wars, take pride in killing people, and enjoy wearing uniforms. I will make sure then that all the countries get this information at the same time. We call this a level playing field, I believe. All being equal, men are intelligent to a degree, and it will be a stalemate in the world arena.

SOLTIS

You are insane if you think you can hide this from us for seventy five years.

DOCTOR MUSTAFA

I have set up banks, accounts, lawyers, trusts, to all release information seventy five years from now. None of the accounts are in my name, nor does any one know what this information is. All have been paid for their services from secret numbered accounts.

LARMON

Enough of this bullshit lets take him where he will tell us everything he knows.

SOLTIS

You may be right Larmon. Reason seems to be lacking in this conversation.

DOCTOR MUSTAFA

I thought I explained it very well as to the phenomenon and what I will do.

SOLTIS

You forgot one simple detail. We three are armed, the house is surrounded by police. In other words we have you by the balls doctor.

DOCTOR MUSTAFA

Look at this chess board on the table gentlemen.

The three army people come around and look at the chess board. The black pieces have most of the pieces on the board the white have only the king and queen.

SOLTIS

Looks like the black have all the pieces.

DOCTOR MUSTAFA

Except now is the white move and the queen checks the black king. The black king is surrounded on every side by his own pieces except the path the queen is checking. None of the Black pieces can block the white queen.

SOLTIS

Enough Doctor, we are leaving.

DOCTOR MUSTAFA

Yes we are certainly leaving general. Before we leave could you call the officers outside and tell them to move away from my house. I wish them no harm. The four of us are going to find out about the God Particles. You have sixty seconds to call the men outside Larmon. The count down is started.

Galvin runs to open door, the door is locked.

DOCTOR MUSTAFA

The door is locked, windows barred, house is now on self destruct count down. Larmon call the men outside.

Larmon dials and yells at the phone

LARMON

Get the fuck away from the house, bomb.

Soltis pulls out his pistol and aims at the doctor.

SOLTIS

Cut the shit out and open the door.

DOCTOR MUSTAFA

Look, as a doctor, I can guarantee it will not hurt and you will be a part of the whole God Particle sea. Any last words general?

The scene ends as the police run away from around the building. Gavin and Larmon try to bust down door and everything disappears in a white flash

SCENE 31

Takes the place in Metcalf's suite at Caesars hotel. Peter is seemingly sleeping on a couch. He is dressed in a tux and has a note in his hands. Janet is trying to wake him up and starts crying. She goes to the phone and calls father Valentine. She wakes him up and tells him that he better cancel his flight home and help her. She tells him Peter chose the option x that he mentioned when they all talked. Soon after the phone call Father Valentine knocks and Janet lets him in.

JANET

He left me father. He went and did this to me.

VALENTINE

Did what?

She now leads him by the hand and shows him Peter laying on the couch.

VALENTINE

What is wrong with him?

JANET

He is gone, out of body traveling somewhere. He did not tell me he was going to do it. How could he do this to me?

VALENTINE

Wake him up.

He reaches over and starts nudging Peter

JANET

I tried for several hours. He is gone.

VALENTINE

Is he dead?

JANET

No and yes, if you can believe that.

VALENTINE

We should call the paramedics, emergency.

JANET

No, read his note.

They both look at the note and Janet reads the note.

JANET

"Dear Janet I am truly sorry for choosing option x. I have decided not to return to my body but as Doctor Mustafa theorized I wish to meld into the God Particle total. The reasons are simple. I do not wish to be a pawn or weapon of the government, I know you do not want the striving suburban type life with me, I also can not live this empty Paris Hilton type existence with you. So I bid you goodbye. I also leave you with many, many, safety deposit boxes full of money so you can live the way you want without any problems. I thank Father Valentine for being a friend and ask one more favor of him. Please get my mortal remains to your family crypt in Resurrection Cemetery in Justice Illinois. Please put me in there. I leave enough money and much more in my pockets to get my body there somehow, car, van, plane, or train. Please do not embalm or cremate my body. You never know I might change my mind. Sorry, and thank you. Peter."

VALENTINE

I think I am dreaming. I will wake up I believe.

JANET

You are not dreaming, this is a real nightmare Peter brought on us.

VALENTINE

He looks like he is sleeping, you checked for life signs?

JANET

There are none, it is like the other out of body travels except this is over the time limit for the return.

VALENTINE

What should we do?

JANET

You stay here with him and call me on my car phone I am going to see Doctor Mustafa to see if he knows how to reverse this absence of Peter's essence.

VALENTINE

I have a hard time believing this. You are sure he is not in some trance?

JANET

I am positive he chose to travel out of body and just simply leave us like this.

She leaves the suite and gets the valet to bring her car, a Porsche, She tips the valet and heads out to the desert, to Mount Charleston to see Dr.Mustafa. The scenic drive down the strip, and into the desert, and the mountains is an impressive drive. She speeds like a demon on the open road. She stops at the information center in Mount Charleston and gets directions to the doctor's house.

She drives the Porsche into the driveway and as she is getting out she sees several police officers running away from the house and yelling at her to get away from the house. She stands confused and then there is a huge explosion, a white flash, and all is gone, house, Porsche, Janet, and only falling rubble and smoke appear.

SCENE 32

Father Valentine tries calling Janet and gets no answer. He is tempted not to do what Peter asked for in the note. He rereads the note several times. Watching the news he hears that a doctor Mustafa's house has blown up in Mount Charleston. The report continues and says that a woman driving a Porsche was also killed by the house. The reporter believes it was a gas explosion. Valentine hearing this decides to do what Peter asked for. He leaves the suite and puts on a do not disturb sign on door knob. Father Valentine gets a cab and is driven to a car dealer where he buys a custom converted van with the cash Peter left. He gets back to the hotel and calls the desk tells them he is checking out and needs a wheel chair in his room for a sick friend. Valentine goes back to his room and packs his suitcase. The wheel chair is brought to his room. He tips the porter. Some moments later he takes the wheel chair up to Metcalf's suite. He struggles to load Peter into the wheel chair then he puts a light blanket around Peter, puts a cap with a big sun visor on his head. He ties Peter to the back of the chair with some belts and the light blanket covers the belts holding Peter in the wheel chair. He puts his small suitcase on Peter's lap and leaves the hotel. He is offered help but turns it down and gets to the van. He now loads peter through a side door in the van and onto a low couch. The van is really super plush. He returns the wheel chair to a parking lot attendant and sets out for Chicago.

SCENE 33

As he is driving through the desert he talks to himself.

Valentine

I must be really crazy to believe any of this. If you start decomposing on me I will know that this is all some sort of insanity you perpetrated on everyone Peter.

SCENE 34

What we see is Valentine buying a coffin in a coffin store.
Valentine is looking at a metal and wood models. A salesman stands looking at him.

SALESMAN

How can I help you father?

VALENTINE

Which one is the lightest one?

SALESMAN

No one has asked me that ever. You intend to travel with it or carry it around.

VALENTINE

My uncles will be pall bearers and the youngest is eighty eight, they are very weak.

SALESMAN

Why not just let them walk next to the coffin, and have some younger people carry it?

VALENTINE

They insist on doing it themselves, you know how old people can get.

SALESMAN

Well the lightest one is the thinnest gage of metal and is the cheapest. Does not seal at all, the handles are stationary and not hinged. The interior is cheap cloth, not the fine silks in the more expensive models. It will not preserve the body very well.

VALENTINE

You would not want to bet on the preservation time in this case.

SALESMAN

Huh?

VALENTINE

I am joking. I will take this one.

SALESMAN

I will write up the paperwork and you can pay now or I can bill you. You can also tell me where to deliver it.

VALENTINE

I will pay cash now and take the coffin in my van.

SALESMAN

Strange as your request is, it is our motto that the customer is always right. We never got a complaint from the ultimate user of our product.

The transaction is completed and the coffin is loaded into the van.

SALESMAN

This is some customized van Father.

VALENTINE

It really belongs to a friend of mine.

SALESMAN

I did not think a priest would own something like this.

Father drives off after saying goodbye.

SCENE 35

He drives to Resurrection Cemetery and parks by his family crypt. He waits by the crypt for a while to see that no one is around and then he drags out the coffin and drags it inside the crypt.

He prays inside and positions the coffin on one of the shelves.

VALENTINE

Please God do not let me be mentally sick. What I am doing is casting some doubts in my mind.

SCENE 36

Valentine now leaves for his parish residence where he has dragged and hidden Peter. Arriving at his residence it is now getting dark and Valentine now carries Peter into the Van and locks the door on the van. He goes back to the residence kneels before the statue of Christ and prays.

VALENTINE
Lord forgive me if this is all wrong, what I have done was at Peter's request.

SCENE 37

Next few days he drives to the cemetery trying to get Peter into the crypt but he gets interrupted by funerals and parishioners he meets. Finally on a rainy day no one is around the crypt and he carries Peter out of the van and takes him inside the crypt and places him in the coffin.

Valentine

What are friends for Peter if not to help one another? What have you talked me into? I would probably be put in a nut house and the key thrown away if this escapade was ever discovered. The only reality I have is the fact that you are still not decomposing.

SCENE 38

This scene goes back to eight years after Peter's disappearance. A young man is driving a sporty car through the cornfields in Illinois. Sitting next to him is a beatiful woman that had claimed years back to have been impregnated by Peter and received money from the Metcalfs.

APRIL

How far is your parent's farm.

ARCHIE

Ten minutes and you will get to meet my parents. By the way please do not tell them what you did for a living years back, lap dancing might not get us off on the right foot with my parents.

APRIL

I know that, let us not talk about that, Jeramy is waking up in the back.

ARCHIE

Hey Jeramy are you up? Time to meet my parents and see the farm. I can not wait to show you all the animals.

Jeramy sits up rubbimg his eyes and says;

JERAMY

Mom I keep having these dreams that it seems I wake up in the dreams in the strangest places. It is weird mom. Why do I dream like that?

SCENE 39

Years go by, and more years go by, Father Valentine is now in his eighties and a futuristic electric taxi drives him up to the crypt with a young girl driver.

DRIVER

How long will you be sir. The GPS will show we are not moving, if I wait for you, I will have to call in and charge you.

VALENTINE

Tell them you will be paid for waiting time. I have to talk to my friend Peter, I mean pray for him, and pray for my wife Marrisa, she is also resting there.

DRIVER

No rush sir, but the meter keeps running you know.

Valentine goes into the crypt and opens Peter's coffin.

VALENTINE

Well hello Peter. Look at you . . . not a day older than when I dragged you into this place some fifty years ago. I have been coming here to have a drink with you every few months and to see if you have been keeping an eye on my Marrisa. You know Peter everything in life is a trade off. You did not decompose month after month, and that destroyed my faith. I started believing in your theory of the God Particle. Today science has established that truly all things that exist are made up of this smallest energy building block. It simply changes into different forms. Possibly the way God is, and thinks, encompassing all that exists. I guess you know, I went back and married Marrisa after I left the priesthood. We had a great life together, filled with love and appreciation of life. You never told me I was in your will if something happened to Janet I got all the safety deposit boxes with your millions after you were officially declared dead, and Janet was identified at doctor Mustafa's house when it blew up. We invested and spent the money helping people, we set up a soup kitchen like you wanted, and Marrisa did a lot of counseling using her psych. degree. How many bottles I drank here, in this crypt, with you, of your favorite Christian Brothers Brandy? I always had hope that when I am here you will wake up someday and tell me what is there after death. You are difficult like always, I guess I will have to wait to find out for myself. I got to tell you another thing happened to me recently. April came to see me some time back and told me that her son started having strange dreams when he was about eight. When he got out of college he went to work for the government on some hush, hush, project as she explained it. I can just imagine what his job is. The boy is your son. I might call him sometime, probably not.

The horn beeps outside and Valentine steps out of the crypt and gets in the taxi.

DRIVER

Sorry to rush you but I have to get you back home and my shift ends soon.

VALENTINE

No problem I will be back here one way or another, if you know what I mean.

The taxi pulls away and there is a shot of it going away from the crypt, a gust of wind picks up a bunch of leaves and swirls them toward the door of the crypt.

The God Particle, a story, a screen play, is about the out of body travel ability, propelling mankind in an evolutionary leap forward or a great step in a better understanding of God.

The protagonists in this story, Peter Metcalf and the two war veterans have experienced real death and been resuscitated and cured with illegal stem cell cocktails and are experiencing astounding side affects that are upsetting all of our legal agencies from the local police precincts to the White house.

Throughout history, in every culture, there were stories, myths, of shape shifting phenomenon and many other impossible to explain occurrences. Vampires, werewolves, zombies, ghosts, witches, and hauntings were all present in our history. The stories and myths were built, and embellished around an original seed of truth that had occurred long ago in all these cases.

The story of The God Particle brings together the old myths in our cultures of the so called psychic phenomenon and ties them all together with a new scientific theory of the Higgs-Bosun, the God Particle theory, that makes the myths seem possibly true.

This scientific theory is that the whole universe is made up of the smallest building blocks, the God Particles, the Higgs-Bosun particles, and that they are constantly changing forms of everything that exists. The accidental side affect for our protagonists propel them into a world of shape shifting out of body experiences.

The God Particle story explains how the ever changing groups of these God Particles shaping different forms can be looked at, as God's Intelligent Design, his way of thinking, and causing evolutionary changes in the universe.

The God Particle story ties science and religion in a new light. Religion must evolve and change to survive. The so called coming Biblical Rapture might be the leap of the whole human race to a higher form, closer to God, on the evolutionary ladder.